To
Th...

DJ Jefferson
2023

Unleashed

Volume 2

Unleashed

Volume 2

E. L. Jefferson

UNLEASHED
Volume 2

Copyright © 2022 by E.L. Jefferson

All rights reserved. No part of this book may be reproduced, stored, or transmitted by any means-whether auditory, graphic, mechanical, or electronic-without written permission of the author, except in the case of brief excerpts used in critical articles and reviews. Unauthorized reproduction of any part of this work is illegal and is punishable by law.

This novel is a work of fiction. Names, characters, places, and incidents either are the product of the author's imagination or are used fictitiously. Any resemblance to actual persons, living or dead is entirely coincidental.

Because of the dynamic nature of the internet, any web addresses or links contained in this book may have changed since publication and may no longer be valid. The views expressed in this work are solely those of the author.

Cover designs by Tovaun McNeil
An E. L. Book
Published by E. L. Books

Library of Congress Control Number: 2022942296
ISBN (paperback): 9781662929809
eISBN: 9781662929816

*We are all responsible for the evil
that exists within each of us, and the consequences
that follow when that evil is let loose upon
the world we all live in.*

1

"A DARK MOTHER," they whispered together, then sat in silence. The coolness of the large subterranean cave was relief from the heat of the South American jungle above. Torchlight reflected on the stone table before them. The three men removed their hoods, and all stared at the one unoccupied seat.

"Shango," Ogun said, "we all share your concern for Damon, and we will address your brother's status during these discussions. We have matters of great import to deal with, at this moment."

"I understand, Ogun," Shango replied to his leader.

"You all know the violent past of our people," Ogun continued, "and that we are responsible for almost annihilating not only ourselves with our warlike ways, but all the lesser hominid species as well. You all are aware that we Proto Sapiens trace our origins back many uncounted millennia, long before the Homo Sapiens crawled out of their caves. What you may not be totally aware of is why."

"What do you mean, Ogun?" Nuru asked. "You are the eldest of the council and the Keeper. You possess knowledge we do not. What are you saying?"

"Many millennia past," Ogun explained, "we were violent, barbaric, warlike, and cruel. Our enhanced abilities, in contrast to the short-lived Homos, helped to spur these tendencies in our kind. We were also many other things. Our kind erected massive, beautiful cities and spread our culture all over our home continent of Africanus. We also developed technologies and governmental systems that succeeded for centuries. Over time, we spread out from the homeland, to the north and far beyond."

Ogun's voice grew in volume, and he struck the stone table with his fist. "As we grew," he cried, "so too did our wars and endless conflicts." In fury, he struck the table again. "With each other—in a never-ending struggle for dominance.

You all know that we Protos destroyed millions of our kind and the others in our senseless wars without end." His eyes flashed. "It was during these times that the first of the ancient mothers appeared. Those who became known as the Dark Ones. They were rarely seen during the day, and they acted through surrogates—just as we do now. However, for reasons not clearly known, they thrived in darkness and led many campaigns after sunset."

Ogun paused, remembering. "They would go on to rule all the ancient houses of every civilization that was to follow. One day, they became those the ancients would call the Dark Mothers. They thrived on death and destruction; their cruelty was boundless. They destroyed whole populations." Ogun stood and began pacing the floor. "Their blood lust passed on to every Proto in existence! Millenia ago, it was a Dark Mother in a foreign land who laid the foundation for the lesser short-lived Homos to rise against our kind, until she was defeated. How that happened the records do not show, but for all their cruelty, it was the Dark Mothers who laid the foundation for our domination of the world—"

"Ogun," Nuru broke in, concerned at Ogun's increasingly disturbed demeanor. "What more can you tell us of these Dark Mothers that once ruled our people?" he asked. "How did they come to be called by that name?"

Calmer now, Ogun replied, "No one knows when the first of the Dark Mothers appeared among our kind, or even how they came to be. Whereas a mother is loving, nurturing, and protective, those who would become known as Dark Mothers were evil incarnate, living only to destroy and kill. They thrived on bloodlust and carnage. It has been written that they were utterly ruthless and without mercy. It is amazing any of us, Proto or Homo, survived under their rule."

Ogun paused again, and then said, "Our ancient records do show, however, that for twenty millennia, the seven ruling houses of the Protos were led by women—all thought to be Dark Mothers. We became a matriarchal civilization, and it was one of our most violent periods. The reign of the Dark Mothers lasted at least twenty thousand years. Far beyond even our own councils."

"Ogun," Shango said, "that still doesn't tell us why they were so feared or why we should be concerned about them now, after all this time. There are no more ruling houses, and even if you somehow sense the presence of one of these Dark creatures, how could that threaten us?"

"I agree with Shango," Nuru said. "Ogun, we of the Council of Elders have controlled the modern world for well over five thousand years. There is no force on the planet that could defeat us."

Ogun shook his head and sighed. "Ordinarily I would agree with you both. And Shango, the word *creature* was indeed an interesting choice. There are accounts in the record of the power of the Dark Mothers. Just as we Protos are both mentally and physically far superior to ordinary Homos, a Dark Mother was said to have abilities far superior to ours. My studies show that they had superior physical strength and true telepathic abilities. They crippled whole armies with just the power of their minds. They slaughtered enemies—and even their own people—with the power of their thoughts. Although I am the Keeper of all knowledge and have the ability of the Mind Touch, my telepathic abilities are limited compared to theirs. Yes, I can sense you of the council anywhere in the world for brief periods, and I can contact any of our people. My mental abilities were honed through centuries of study and meditation, but my abilities only work with other Protos. A Dark Mother had no such limitations.

"Just as our physical abilities are genetic, so too a Dark Mother's ability may have been the result of a genetic mutation among our kind. However, I think this unlikely, because if this were the case, the Dark Ones would still be among us. I believe that they were somehow bred among our kind, because there were not many of them in our long history. I do not know for certain."

Ogun paused again, lost in thought. "A Dark Mother," he resumed, "could control both Protos and Homos, whereas my Mind Touch doesn't work with Homos. The Dark Ones had true telekinetic abilities and were capable of destroying with a thought. I do not know the origins of their abilities, and my research continues, but the records I have studied are clear and infallible. They show that the most powerful of the Dark Mothers had what was called the power of shadow. This was the most devastating power of those who possessed it, for it gave them the ability to physically merge with either a shadow or a darkened space, or even the night itself, rendering them invisible for all intents and purposes." He gazed intently at Nuru and Shango. "You can imagine the tremendous advantage this would have afforded anyone with this power. It has been written that a Dark Mother could suddenly appear out of nowhere and destroy dozens of people with her bare hands, crossing vast distances in darkness as if she had teleported. To those who knew them, a Dark Mother's powers seemed almost mystical. Combined with her innate intelligence, a Dark Mother was truly a formidable foe." Ogun, his explanation complete, took his seat again.

Nuru, in awe of Ogun's recounting, asked, "Could these abilities be the result of some type of transmutation or experimentation?"

"I do not know," Ogun replied, "but I have learned that there were only twelve known accounts of ruling Dark Mothers in our history. The last known Dark Mother ruled over seven thousand years ago. Well before our age of enlightenment, and our conquest of the world as it is today."

Shango now spoke up. "Ogun, we know that mysticism is crap. It was we who instilled the idea in the Homos for thousands of years. However, does the record show what happened to any of these so-called Dark Mothers? For all their abilities, were their lifespans comparable or superior to ours? And could these Dark Mothers be killed?"

"I cannot answer that question without more information," Ogun replied, "but I'd speculate that—based on our own physiology—the Dark Mothers would have had shorter natural lifespans than our own. Our natural lifespan is approximately thirty-five hundred years. If their abilities were natural and they had a similar physiology to ours, then the strain of those abilities on their systems would have been enormous and would possibly have shortened their lifespans. Could they be killed? The answer is yes. But with the abilities they had, it would be extremely difficult compared to killing baseline Protos. I have found four accounts of Dark Mothers being killed in battle—but all by opposing Dark Mothers."

"Ogun," Shango asked, his voice now filled with trepidation, "while we are difficult to kill, we have access to far superior weaponry than is available to the planet's general population. Even if this presence you sense does turn out to be an awakening Dark Mother, or something similar, can't we destroy it before it threatens us?"

"Possibly," Ogun answered. "If we can locate it. If this is an awakening Dark Mother in our era, then she could destroy us all. That is, if the power I sensed is allowed to grow further, but I also sense it is still weak and undeveloped. Whatever this presence is, I touched its mind. Therefore, it is a danger to us all and must be destroyed."

"Ogun," Shango objected, "first of all, we don't know that this thing is a Dark Mother. Second, if it is, then where did it come from? And, more importantly, are they born, as we are, with these abilities? Or are they somehow cultivated as the child grows?"

"All interesting questions, Shango," Ogun mused. "You are correct. I don't know if this thing I sense is a Dark Mother, but whatever it is, its power could threaten us all. We must prepare ourselves for the possibility." He stared at the two elders. "We have time on our side, since whatever this presence is, it is unaware of our kind. Nothing in my experience, short of the power of a Dark Mother, could have triggered my senses. The Dark Ones could very well be born with the innate abilities we have discussed, but this kind of power must be cultivated and refined over time. If not, such an individual could easily destroy all those around them, leaving a wake of destruction in their path.

"This possibility could work to our advantage," Ogun mused. "If a Proto had been born with these powers, the child would have been destroyed long before its power could grow."

"I know what you all are thinking," Ogun said. "No Proto would harm another, but such a child could not be allowed to exist. I would have become aware of a Proto with such abilities. Homos have never produced offspring with anywhere near our own abilities. Their lifespans are far too short. There may be billions of them to our millions, but this world belongs to us!"

"I understand now why this is of grave concern to us all, Ogun," Nuru said.

"A Dark Mother—or anyone with this kind of power must be destroyed at all costs," Ogun insisted, his voice rising in anger. "They could possibly become aware of us and turn the entire population against our kind. We cannot allow that to happen."

"How do we find this creature, Ogun?" Shango asked.

"I will have to focus my mind to detect the slightest manifestation of its abilities," Ogun replied. "Once I do that, I will be better able to get a fix on its location."

"Ogun," Shango asked, "can only female Protos have these abilities?"

"Yes," Ogun replied. "According to everything I've studied thus far, only females of our kind possessed the abilities of a Dark Mother."

"When you first became aware of its presence," Nuru said, "from where in the world did the impressions emanate?"

"When I first became aware of its presence, it was close," Ogun said. "It was in Damon's territory. Somewhere in the southern portion of North America. The third time I sensed its power, I felt that its energy had changed. It had grown proportionately stronger, but like the previous times, it abruptly faded, as if a switch had turned it off. I was able to determine, without a doubt, that Nuru's territories of Africa and Australia were not the source. Nor were Shango's territories of the Middle East, Europe, and Asia. I haven't detected any emanations from my territories of Central and South America. Whatever—or whoever—is generating this force is definitely located in Damon's territory."

"The goddamn USA," Shango said with disgust. "I should have guessed."

"This brings us back to Damon," Ogun interjected. "Damon is not dead, Shango."

"You said earlier that you couldn't sense his mind," Shango reminded him.

"That is true," Ogun admitted, "but at the time I deemed it necessary to call you both here, I was trying to track down the source of the presence I had sensed. I would know if Damon was dead. He is not. I have linked you three directly to me with my Mind Touch. If Damon were dead, I would have felt him die. Which means, for the last few months, he has been possibly incapacitated and/or unable to contact us for some reason. Otherwise, he would have responded using his commlink. I have already put out a query to every hospital and medical facility within a five-hundred-mile radius surrounding Damon's last known location in the Washington DC metropolitan area. I have our people running computer searches using every local, state, and federal database at their disposal. All surrounding law enforcement agencies have been notified, and our people have assured me that they will find him."

The three men now stood up, their impressive six feet six inch tall frames towering over the table.

Shango turned to face Ogun. "As in all matters, you are aware of all things, Ogun. I apologize for my earlier outburst." *I will find this thing myself and rip its fucking head off its shoulders if I have to.*

Ogun looked intently at Shango, placing both his hands on the man's shoulders. "I understand how you feel, brother," he said. "Your emotions betray you. You and your brother's contempt for the Homos is well known to me. However, until we understand what we are dealing with, you will take no such action unless I authorize it. Do you understand?"

"Yes, Ogun," Shango replied. *That damn telepathy.*

"We will bring your brother home to us."

"In the meantime, Ogun," Nuru said, "if we start with the southern states, we need to begin monitoring for the source of this power. How shall we proceed?"

"Let us go to my Operations Room," Ogun replied.

THEY WALKED OUT of the cavernous meeting chamber and down a dimly lit passageway, their boots echoing on the ancient and massive stones lining the passageway. The stones soon gave way to walls of smooth concrete and steel. The group stopped at two large doors. Each door bore two 12 × 12 inch electronic palm readers. Each palm reader glowed red as the men stood before them. Shango, standing to Ogun's left, placed his right hand on the leftmost reader. Ogun placed both his palms on the two middle readers, and Nuru placed his right hand on the remaining reader. Above the men, a panel in the ceiling silently opened and three silver cylinders began to glow.

An electronic voice spoke. *"State your identity."*

"Shango the Destroyer."

"Ogun the Keeper."

"Nuru the Builder."

The ceiling panel above the men silently slid shut, and the bright red light of the readers faded. The massive metal doors retreated into the walls.

The three men walked into the vast room before them, and the doors shut behind them. Hundreds of huge electronic monitors glowed and blinked on every wall, as far as the eye could see. The vast chamber was astonishing in size. At its center, a floor to ceiling array of computers stretched over one hundred yards in length. The room contained no workers, and even with the vast amount of automated electronic equipment in the chamber, the room was dead silent until the three figures began to speak.

"I am awed every time I walk into this chamber, Ogun," Nuru said. "It is most impressive. I trust that the new fusion reactor located beneath this complex is functioning as designed?"

"It is indeed," Ogun replied, "and I would expect no less from Nuru the Master Builder. Even still, my complex is not much more impressive than your own operation monitoring stations, and we are all linked via satellite."

"That may be so," Shango said, "but this is still an impressive sight."

Ogun pointed ahead. "Let us go to my command center, where we can continue our discussion and if you wish you may monitor your own systems."

The three men walked past the array of computers. Arriving at an elevator, they rode it to the walkway five stories above the floor of the chamber. Emerging from the elevator, they briefly stood overlooking the sea of monitors and computers below them. They then headed for Ogun's command center, removed their robes, and each sat facing an array of sixteen large monitors, grouped in sets of four, aligned vertically. Again, the seat left empty did not go unnoticed by any of them.

"I am currently monitoring the activities of these so-called world leaders and their governing bodies," Ogun announced. "The US Senate and House of Representatives debating to no end. We made the right choice when we installed that idiot as US president. Look at him sitting behind his desk, looking like a lost child. He doesn't have a clue as to what he is doing, and he is as pliable as putty.

Now the only question is do we let him remain as the president or do we get rid of him after we have him start the next world war. That would be a fitting query for the council's strategist if he were present. Until we identify and eliminate the presence I sense, all other priorities are rescinded."

"The British Parliament is in session at the moment, debating Brexit," Ogun stated.

"We will allow them to leave," Shango said, "as that will further destabilize that region. I have already given the order, and the current issues surrounding their newly elected leader will prove a further distraction." Shango smirked. "The German Prime Minister is also being taken to a meeting in Frankfurt, as we speak, to meet with the French president to discuss their Russian problem. Which we haven't revealed to the world yet."

"As we can see on the monitors," Nuru indicated, "Putin's arrogance knows no bounds. While his country's people are starving and miserable, he gets out of his heated swimming pool every morning, dons a robe, and inspects the cases of foreign currency his personal guards bring him every morning. These billions he deposits in his personal accounts every day—or so he believes. When the source of this currency has been revealed to the world, every nation on the planet will scream for his death. Everything is proceeding as scripted."

"We will let these events play out, for the time being," Ogun said. "Our surrogates will keep our current plans on course. We must now turn our attention to finding the source of the presence I've been sensing and destroy it."

"It is your belief that this thing presents that great a threat to us, Ogun?" Nuru asked.

"It is not a belief, brother," Ogun responded. "It is a fact. If this thing is indeed a Dark Mother—or an awakening force analogous to one—we must destroy it before it can grow stronger. Before it becomes aware of our kind. According to the ancient records, a Dark Mother does not follow. It conquers. Dark Mothers do not seek council; they destroy. They annihilate all in their path, leaving rivers of blood in their wake, until their domination is complete."

"If these creatures are indeed the agents of destruction and chaos, as told in our history," Shango mused, "then tracking it in the modern world should be fairly easy. If killing and destruction are hallmarks of these creatures, then it would kill and destroy with impunity if left unchecked, leaving a trail to follow."

"Explain your reasoning, Shango," Nuru said.

"We know that whatever this thing is," Shango explained, "it is currently located somewhere in the southern portion of the US, hidden among the millions that reside in that sector of the country. Until Ogun can pinpoint its exact location, all we need do is: first, focus our attention on the region from Texas to Georgia. Suspend all chaos activity in that sector until we are sure it's either not there or until we can contain and destroy it."

"An excellent stratagem, Shango," Ogun replied, "but to implement that ploy over such a wide sector of the country is a massive undertaking and not without risk. To do so in a city or even in a whole state is achievable. While we have the means to do as you suggest, it would require considerably more resources than required for containing a city or a single state."

Shango smiled. "I suggested that we suspend all major chaos operations in that sector, not all criminal activity. The Homos have to be kept busy and distracted. We already have access to every cell phone and electronic camera on the planet, so now we focus our attention on that sector's eyes and ears. The mass killings, shootings, bombings, all domestic terrorist operations, hate-group operations, gang-related operations, Internet propaganda, drug-related operations, and all diversionary criminal operations. Those we cease for now. We divert and analyze all cell phone activity through our systems, focusing on major pandemonium conditions not of our implementation. We limit all media coverage to all but local low-level disturbances. We will also have no law enforcement interference with this thing's activities, when it does show itself. This way, when our problem rears its head and begins to massacre the Homos, all we need do is follow the trail right to it. And then we dispatch our K squads." Shango smiled again.

"Excellent, Shango!" Ogun said. "Let us implement that plan now."

The three elders stood, and each walked to a designated multi-screened computer complex, initiating the extensive work to implement the plan to capture an unknown force that even they had come to fear.

2

THE CLUB, THE CLASSIC, was one of the most popular, most well-patronized night clubs in the New Orleans area. Out in the suburbs, it was away from the crowded nightlife district of the city. The club attracted a more affluent crowd of professionals than most of the city's other night spots. In the seclusion of the suburbs, the sophisticated clientele at this club could enjoy the privacy to indulge in not only high-priced cuisine and alcohol, but high-priced drugs as well.

A tall, stunning woman dressed in black left the ladies' room and walked down a crowed corridor to return to her seat at the bar. She passed the other women standing on either side of the corridor snorting coke, and they all took notice.

"Ashley, have you ever seen her here before?" Chloe asked her friend.

"Someone who looks like her I would have noticed," Ashley replied, "so she must be a new face."

"She's very pretty," Chloe noted, "but there's an air of arrogance about her. Did you notice that she walked by everyone as if she didn't even see us? Like her black ass is somehow better than us? She isn't the only pretty woman in the building," Chloe added, with annoyance.

"Is someone a little jealous? Ashley teased.

"No, I'm not."

"Coke is supposed to make you mellow, Chloe, not stress you out. Forget her. You know men can't resist those big blue eyes of yours, and that blond hair." Ashley laughed.

"Next to her, I don't know," Chloe said with a grimace.

THE SUBJECT OF their brief conversation returned to her seat at the bar. Everyone she passed had taken notice of her. Heads at every table had turned in her direction. Women at those tables had given angry looks to the men seated with them, as the men had gawked at Raven as she passed.

The bar was busy, and the bartender stopped making a cocktail for another guest and turned his full attention to the woman who just sat down. The waiting guest noticed, but the bartender ignored him.

"Raven, would you like another glass of Dom Perignon?" the bartender asked, failing to quell the eagerness in his voice.

"I would. Thank you, Max," she replied.

The bartender turned to retrieve the bottle, only to find it was empty. "I'll be right back," he said. "I have to get another chilled bottle from the back." He started to walk away, but the irritated customer now spoke.

"Excuse me," the patron said. "She is not the only goddamned customer here. Can you please make my drink? I was here first!"

"Alex," Max called to his follow bartender, "can you make this guy a Long Island? I have to go to the chiller."

"Sure thing, Max. I got it."

"No, I was here before her," the patron complained. "I want *him* to make my damn drink. He had the gall to stop making my shit to wait on her."

"Look, sir. I'll make the drink now," Alex said. "Max had to go to the chiller."

"He would have had my order taken care of if he hadn't stopped to wait on her."

Alex sighed, trying to compose himself before responding to the angry man. "I'll have your Long Island ready in a few seconds, sir."

"Just who the hell does she think she is?" The customer pointed in Raven's direction, making sure she could hear him over the music playing in the background. He stared at Raven from across bar. The atmosphere became tense.

RAVEN RETURNED his stare, winked at him, and allowed a slight smile to form on her face.

This infuriated him. He walked toward her.

"Sir, your drink is ready." Alex called out, as the man got closer to Raven. He surreptitiously pressed the panic button under the bar counter.

The man stopped one seat away from Raven. She remained seated.

"Just who the fuck do you think you are, goddamnit?" he demanded. "I don't care what you look like. Do you know who I am?"

She turned toward the angry guest. "Your anger is misplaced," she said. "Don't make your problem mine. I am trying to enjoy a glass of champagne; it is a very refreshing drink. As to who you are? I would guess an intoxicated idiot who can't control himself when he drinks. In any case, who you are is of no significance to me whatsoever. It would be best if you took your drink and returned to wherever it was you were seated."

"You have a smart damn mouth, don't you? If I don't, just what the hell are you gonna do about it?"

Raven stood to face the angry man. The bar manager and Max now approached the two.

Raven spoke in a low tone that only she and the man could hear. "All right. How about this? Please do something stupid that would give me a reason to kill you where you stand." She smiled.

"I know you didn't just threaten me!"

"I did indeed. And I look forward to our next encounter," she replied.

"Did you hear what this bitch said to me?" the man yelled in a loud angry voice.

Raven sat down.

"All right, Trevor, that's enough," the bar manager shouted in a loud voice. "Take your drink and return to your seat, or I'll have you removed."

The man looked over to see who had spoken, took the offered drink, and started to walk away. "This isn't over, bitch," he said. "I'll see you again."

"I apologize for that, ma'am," the bar manager said, extending his hand to Raven and she accepted it. "I'm Russell, the bar manager. His behavior was inexcusable. We don't tolerate that kind of behavior here, and he will not be getting in here again."

Max placed a glass of champagne in front of Raven.

"This is on me," Russell said. "I'm sorry. I didn't get your name?"

"Raven is my name."

"Excellent. A fitting name for such a beautiful woman. Please enjoy yourself, Raven, and if you need anything, please let me know."

"I will, Russell. Thank you."

ON THE OTHER SIDE of the bar, near the front entrance, a table of five friends had started to wonder what had happened to their missing companion.

"Has anybody seen Carla?" Barbara asked.

"She went to try to talk to that pretty bitch at the bar, the one dressed in black," Mya replied. "The one everybody is trying not to look at. Carla followed her down coke alley toward the ladies' room, and that's the last time I saw her. Maybe she hooked up with some other bitch."

"What the fuck," Traci said, "Ya'll, Carla is a big girl who can take care of herself. Obviously, she didn't book the bitch at the bar because she not sitting with her."

"I keep trying to tell Carla she can't have everything she sees," Mya said. "She worse than dudes are. She wants to fuck every bitch she looks at. One day, that shit gonna get her dyke ass in big trouble."

"What you mean one day?" Princey asked. "Carla been damn near knocked the fuck out at least four times I know of for hitting on other people's women. She'll do that dumb shit in front of the guys they with. She lucky we got her back, 'cause I don't mind fuckin' somebody up like the last time we had to beat a bitch down."

Barbara chuckled. "Ruben is at the bar right now, scheming on how he can walk out of here wit' that bitch. Since I been sitting here, she hasn't danced with anybody, and all the guys who approached her must a been dissed because she still sittin' by herself. Ruben's cute, but he ain't getting' none of that pussy tonight. It ain't gonna happen. Carla will take care of him though. She a dyke that like suckin' dick. I don't get that one, but she always blowin' Ruben. She says she just don't like to swallow."

"Come on, ya'll," said Mya. "The hell with all that. That shit is between them two. We know all about it, so can we just get our drink on and forget the dumb shit? I just wanna have a good time tonight, and I don't feel like fighting anybody right now."

RAVEN FINISHED her glass of champagne and placed a new one-hundred-dollar bill on the counter.

"Raven, would you like another glass of champagne?" Max asked.

"No, thank you, Max. I think it's time for me to leave."

"I hope that incident with that drunk asshole is not the reason you're leaving. But I have to warn you, Raven. He is a very dangerous person. He's a bigtime drug dealer. In this area, even the cops are afraid of him."

Raven smiled. "Not at all. He would have been no problem at all. I kill problems like that very easily."

Max laughed. "Let me get your change. I'll be right back."

"No, Max. You keep it."

"Thank you, Raven. You take care of yourself and please come back." He took the bill and walked to the cash register.

She stood to walk away.

"Hey, you aren't leaving so soon, are you?" she heard a voice say. "It's still so early."

"Yes, I am." She spoke without facing the speaker.

"Is there anything I can do that would make you stay?"

She turned to look him up and down, before she replied, "No, there is not."

"Can I at least buy you a nightcap before you leave?"

"That would accomplish nothing," she said. "I have a long walk to get home, and I don't need you to buy me anything. You really need to learn to take no for an answer. It will extend your life."

Her reply put a stunned look on his face. "That was cold, Damn, girl. I'm just trying to be friendly."

"I am obviously not a girl. I don't need friends and cold is your friend in the ladies' room. Goodnight." She turned and walked toward the door.

"Can I get you a drink sir?" Max asked.

"Yeah, let me get a Long Island." *Damn that bitch is mean. Fuck was she talking about? 'Cold is your friend in the ladies' room.'* He took his drink and returned to his table.

Raven paused as she got near the exit, turned toward Ruben's table, and smiled at those seated there.

"No luck with that Ruben?" Barbara teased. "That bitch is pretty, but something about her is creepy as hell, too."

"Nah, she blew me off like I was nothing. Oh, well. She's not the only woman in here, but you can't blame a brother for trying. She did say some crazy shit though. Fuck it. No big deal.

"I'm tired of waiting for Carla," Princey said. "Let's order our food. I'm hungry."

RAVEN WALKED OUT of the club and into the darkness. The air was comfortably warm, and there were no other people outside the club. She took note that the parking lot of the establishment was full. She headed for the roadway, but she heard footsteps approaching and a voice called out to her.

"Hey, you!" An angry male voice shouted out. "We have some unfinished business."

Raven stopped walking but did not face the person speaking.

"Bitch," the voice yelled, "Look at me when I'm talking to you."

The man caught up to Raven and turned to face her. He was slightly taller than her, and she saw the hatred in his eyes. She also noted the other man, who stood a few feet behind the man speaking. She smiled.

"You think this is funny, bitch? I'll deal with Russell later. Right now, I'm gonna teach you a lesson."

"Oh, and just what would this lesson be?" Raven asked. "I think he called you Trevor, is it? Do you see me trembling, you white, drunk, imbecile?" Raven stood as still as a statue as she faced him.

"I'm gonna kick the shit out of you then we're gonna take turns fuckin' you up your ass."

Raven threw her head back as she laughed.

Enraged, Trevor pulled back his fist. "Let's see you laugh after I knock out your fucking teeth."

She stopped the blow several inches from her face with her left hand. The impact made a sharp smacking sound, and she held on to his fist. "Is there a problem Trevor?" she asked.

He began to tremble and reached for his right hand. His fist was caught tight in the vice of Raven's hand.

"On your knees, cretin," she commanded. "You have given me cause to destroy you and die you will." She forced him downward.

"Ah! Bitch, let go of my goddamn hand!" He stifled his scream.

His companion moved to attack her from the opposite side. "Let him go, you black—" Raven viciously backhanded her attacker. Blood and teeth flew from his mouth and he fell to his knees.

"What the fuck? Ahhh!" Trevor looked up at Raven and screamed.

She pulled him with her as she moved toward her other would-be attacker and grabbed him by his throat. "Trevor," she said, "I'll make his death agonizing, but he'll die quickly. What is his name? His throat feels so good in my hand. I'll crush his trachea and let him choke and suffocate on his own blood and vomit." She tightened her grip on the man's throat until his eyes bled and began to bulge out of their sockets. After a few seconds, she tossed him to the ground like a bag of garbage.

Through his pain, Trevor was horrified at what he just witnessed.

"I asked you his name," Raven repeated.

On his knees Trevor could barely speak.

"The cracking sound you hear," Raven announced, "are the bones in your hand snapping. Don't you dare scream."

Tears fell down his face with the agony of his fingers being crushed as her hand closed tighter.

"Mar . . . Mar . . . Ah! Marco's his name."

"Somehow, that seems fitting. Now, Trevor, before you die, what is it you do for a living and who exactly are you?"

"I . . . I . . . sell coke, sell coke." He screamed out his agony.

In one motion, Raven released his crushed fist and grabbed him by the throat. "So," she hissed, "you are a drug dealer. I'm sure no one will miss one more like you, Trevor. I will be happy to rid the earth of one such as you." She bent slightly toward his head. "Trevor, before you die, I have one last question for you. What did you drive here tonight? A bigtime, badass drug dealer must have an expensive car?" She loosened her grip on his throat so he could speak.

"BMW M5," he gasped, before Raven again abruptly cut off his air.

"That's good, Trevor." She sneered. "Now, I'm sure you must have some loose change somewhere in that very expensive car that you worked so very hard to acquire. Please tell me where I can find it."

He looked into her eyes, terrified. Her hand squeezed his throat some more.

"What . . . what are you? In da truck, you can have. The key in . . . my pocket . . . please let me go."

"I think I understand what you are trying to say," Raven said. "It's hard to talk when you have a vice around your throat. I must decline your request. However, I'll tell you this: you will receive a death worthy of one such as yourself." She showed him the index finger of her right hand. Holding him by his throat, and with lightning speed, she stabbed out both his eyes. She dropped him to the ground and took the key from his pocket.

A BLOOD CURDLING scream erupted from the ladies' restroom inside the club. The woman ran out the restroom as if her life depended on it.

"What the fuck!" she screamed. "There's a dead girl in there!" She ran down the corridor know as coke alley. Other women went in behind her, and a chorus of screams erupted from the corridor. Every patron in the club turned in that direction, to see women run out screaming and heading for the door.

The club manager quickly moved against the flow of frightened patrons and down the hall. The music had stopped and the anxiety level of the people inside the club now intensified.

"What the fuck is going on?" Princey asked. "Are these bitches trippin' or what?".

"I don't know," Barbara answered. "Did someone say a dead girl is in the ladies' room?"

"Where the fuck is Carla?" Ruben inquired.

"Ruben," Barbara ordered, "go down there and see what the fuck is going on."

Ruben immediately got up and rushed toward the ladies' room, against the flow of people leaving the club. He ran down coke alley toward the ladies' room, followed by a few other men, but they were confronted by one of the club's security men.

"Hold up. I can't let you go in there," the well-muscled security guard said. "We have a situation."

"A situation?" Ruben cried. "One of my friends I came in here with is missing from the group. I need to know if she's in there!"

Russell emerged from the ladies' room. He looked directly at Ruben. "It's Carla. She's dead."

"The fuck you mean? She's dead?" Ruben yelled. "I gotta see her, man!" Tears fell from his face.

"It's okay, Bobby," Russell said. "Let him pass. That was his friend. I'll walk him in. I already called the police. Don't let anybody else down here. Get on the radio, and have Bruce make an announcement that the club is closed now. Get everyone out of here."

"Come on, Ruben," Russell said. They walked into the ladies' room and toward the stall where the body had been found. Russell held onto Ruben's shoulder.

"Oh, fuck!" Ruben cried. "Carla! What the fuck happened, man? That's my girl Carla! What the fuck happened!" He fell to his knees, but then quickly jumped up again and ran to pick up his dead friend.

Russell stopped him. "Ruben, stop! I know she's your friend, but you can't touch her. The police—"

"Fuck the motherfuckin' police! That's my girl in there on the fuckin' floor!" Tears streamed down Ruben's face.

"I know that, but you can't move her body!" Russell pushed Ruben out of the ladies' room. "I'm sorry, Ruben," he said, holding up his hands. "I am, but we have to wait and let the police do their job."

Ruben screamed at the top of his voice, his anger and sadness overwhelming him simultaneously. Many seconds later, he walked down the corridor wiping tears from his face and headed back to his friends. The women saw him and instantly knew something was horribly wrong.

"Ruben! What the fuck is going—" Seeing his eyes, Barbara stopped in mid-sentence.

"It's Carla," Ruben sobbed. "She's dead. It's her in there..."

"Get the fuck outta here," Traci cried. "You bullshittin', Ruben! Don't play fuckin' games like that!"

"I'm telling you," Ruben said. "I saw her on the floor! She's dead!"

"What the fuck happened?" Barbara cried. The woman stood up from the table and looked at Ruben.

"I don't fuckin' know what happened," he said, "but whoever did this shit was here and that motherfucker is going to pay."

Tears began to fall down the faces of the women.

"Wait a fuckin' minute!" Ruben said out loud, to no one. "*'Cold is your friend in the ladies' room.'* It was that bitch at the bar! She said that to me at the bar! It didn't make fuckin' sense at the time, so I just blew it off."

"What the fuck did she say?" Barbara demanded.

"Before that bitch left the bar," Ruben cried, "she said 'cold is your friend in the ladies' room.' I didn't know what the fuck she was talking about. But now—" His words stopped as he again stared into nothingness.

"You think that bitch killed Carla, Ruben?" Mya asked.

"That bitch did look our way when she left," Barbara recalled, "with a fucked-up look on her face."

"That bitch said something else... she said she was walking home," Ruben said. He was interrupted by more screams that came from outside.

"Walking?" Princey said. "Let's go get that bitch. Ruben, you got your gun?" Tears of anger dripped down her face.

"Yeah," Ruben answered. "I'm gonna blow her fuckin' head off."

"Not until I cut her fuckin' throat from ear to ear, Barbara said, wiping away tears.

THE GROUP MOVED to the club's exit. Once more, screams emanated from outside, from the far end of the parking lot. The group ignored the commotion happening around them and followed Ruben to his SUV at the opposite end of the lot. Inside the vehicle, Ruben opened his glovebox, took out the semi-automatic handgun, and stuffed it in the front of his pants. The women all took out knives and straight razors from their handbags.

"Which way do you think that bitch went?" Barbara asked.

"I don't know," Ruben said, "but the entrance to this place is about a thousand feet off the main road. That road splits left and right from there, and then there's nothing around but woods for miles in both directions, so that bitch couldn't have got too far on foot. We gonna search till we find that bitch." He floored the accelerator, and the vehicle sped off down the road.

Anger and bloodlust overpowered the vehicle's occupants. "That bitch is gonna die tonight," Ruben vowed, to no one. A glance to the right revealed police lights flashing in the distance.

"Ruben," Mya said, "try turning left first at the stop sign. The cops are coming from the right off the highway. We can go down that way for a while because there are houses and shit off the main road this way. The highway is to the right, after a mile, and there's nothing else that way."

Ruben aimed the car full speed down the unlit stretch of road into the darkness in search of retribution. "Ya'll take all your shit off," he ordered. "When we catch this bitch, we gonna fuck her up."

The women removed their jackets and other loose-fitting clothing they had on. They also removed any jewelry and watches.

"We ready," Princey said, the anger in her voice barely repressed. "Let's find this bitch."

Minutes passed as the SUV sped down the dark road. Just beyond the range of the car's headlights, another vehicle became visible on the shoulder of the road. Its lights were off. They sped past the vehicle in search of their prey.

"Yo, Ruben," said Princey. "Slow down a little. Don't crash this mothafucka before we catch this bitch."

"Don't worry," Ruben advised. "I got this." The vehicle slowed only slightly, as he negotiated a long S-curve in the road. The SUV negotiated a small hump in the road, and a figure suddenly loomed in the distance. Ruben slowed and turned on his high beams, but then dimmed them and slowed again.

A woman dressed in black was walking in the middle of the road.

"That's that bitch right there." Barbara shouted, pointing at the woman.

"That bitch killed my fuckin' girl!" Ruben yelled. "I'm gonna splatter that bitch all over the fuckin' road." He pressed the accelerator pedal to the floor. The engine roared, slamming the occupants into their seats.

"Yeah! Run that bitch over!" Princey shouted.

Within seconds, the huge SUV was just feet away from impact with the walking woman. Then it was past the point where the woman was walking. Its tires screeched to a halt, leaving a trail of rubber on the road.

Ruben pulled to the side of the road, stopped the engine, and turned off the lights. Everyone got out and walked to the front of the SUV. The full moon dimly shone on the vehicle.

"What the fuck?" Ruben shouted. "Where'd that bitch go? It's like she just disappeared."

"I saw you run over the bitch!" Barbara exclaimed, in disbelief. "I was sitting in the front seat! I saw it all!"

"I didn't feel the car run over that bitch," Traci said. "We shoulda felt something."

"Maybe the car is too heavy for us to feel her get crushed under it?" Mya replied.

Mya peered at the grill of the SUV. "Shit," she said. "It's too dark out here to see much of anything on the car. I can't even tell if it's dented."

"Fuck it," Ruben said. "Her ass coulda been knocked a hundred feet away from the car. Everybody spread the fuck out and see if we can find her body." He took out his gun and led the way. The women took out their weapons and walked behind him.

"Mya, come with me," Traci ordered. "We'll look on this side of the road.

"We'll take the other side of the road," Ruben said, "because her ass is not in the middle of the street. I can see that. If ya'll see anything, holler out. We gotta do this shit quick." He, Barbara, and Princey crossed the two-lane road and walked away from his vehicle.

"TRACI," MYA ASKED, "what do you wanna do to that bitch if we find her first?"

Traci glared. "If the bitch ain't dead, I'm gonna shove my knife right up her pussy, while you cut up that pretty black face of hers—if it's not already fucked up."

"The shit works for me." Mya replied. They walked further down the dark roadside.

A crackling sound alerted Mya. "Traci, did you hear that?"

"Hear what? I didn't hear shit. Just keep walking and look for the bitch's body."

A soft, seductive voice said, "Are you two lovely ladies looking for me?"

The voice came from the darkness in front of the women. They both looked in the direction from which they thought it came.

It spoke again. "I can see you," it said. "Can you see me? I'm standing near the big tree to your right. Come and avenge your dead friend—if you can."

"Right there!" Traci shouted. "I see that bitch!" She pointed her knife toward a half silhouette of a woman's body moving against the tree. Traci and Mya rushed toward it.

"Hey ya'll! We fou—" Mya's shout to her companions was abruptly cut off.

Traci turned toward her friend. Instead, in the dim moonlight, she saw the woman in black, holding Mya off the ground by her neck.

"I believe you two are looking for me?" the woman asked.

Traci was momentarily stunned by the sight before her, but quickly regained her nerve. "Put her the fuck down right now, bitch!" Traci replied, holding out her knife at arm's length.

"I don't see a reason why I should do that, little one. I do believe you said you wanted to shove that small blade of yours up my pussy, while this one destroyed my face. Interesting dynamic isn't it, when the hunters become the hunted. Your friend can't join the conversation, as she is in great peril at the moment. Being held so high off the ground by her neck makes it impossible for her to speak. I can hold her like this for hours—or I can let her go. You need to tell her to stop kicking so much. Yes, she can still hear you. Kicking her legs will only increase her agony. Ha! She just pissed herself." With her little finger, she indicated the knife Traci was holding. "You need only drop your knife, and I will let your friend go."

Traci watched in stunned horror as Mya, held by her neck many feet off the ground, kicked her legs. In a quivering voice, she pleaded, "Mya, stop kicking! Stop! Stop kicking!" She let her knife fall to the ground. "Okay, I dropped the fucking knife!" she yelled, tears falling down her face. "Now let her go."

"As you wish."

With a sickening cracking sound, Mya's body went limp. It made a low thudding sound when it hit the ground.

In a state of terror, Traci reached for the knife she had dropped. A hand forced her head to the ground.

"You didn't really believe that I'd let her live, did you?" the voice teased. "I'm sure you realize by now that I am going to kill you—and all your friends. Just as I enjoyed killing your friend in the ladies' room at that club. I gave her an opportunity to walk away, but her carnal nature wouldn't allow her to. You see, I have no interest in sexual encounters. You should never have come after me. I'm glad you did, though." The woman turned Traci over, pinned her arms to the ground using her knees, and sat on her chest. She placed her hand over Traci's mouth and bent close to her ear.

"I do so enjoy killing," she murmured. "The same way you enjoy the drugs you smoke. I don't care who I kill, as long as I get my fill. Now, I don't care for making a bloody mess. I prefer clean quick kills, like your friend and the hillbillies who tried to pick me up on the road back there. I left their broken and bloody bodies on the side of the road for the world to see. One of those idiots had the nerve to approach me with his little penis in his hand. I ripped it from his body and stuffed it down his friend's throat. What do you think of that?" She chuckled. "Oh, by the way, I can hear your other friends. They are close by, and they are very angry."

Her eyes wide with fright, Traci was frozen with terror. She was going to die, and there was nothing she could do to stop it.

"Now," the woman continued, "you said you were going to shove a sharp object into my body. Specifically, between my legs. That is so unladylike, but then you are no lady, and neither am I. Looking at you now, I do believe you would have done just that if given the chance." She paused to look at Traci. "Oh, poor baby, don't cry now. All the tears in the world won't save you now. I told you I hate making a mess, but I'm going to let you experience how it feels to have something sharp shoved in that part of your body. Believe me, you will not enjoy it. Before we get that intimate though, you should at least know my name. It's Raven." She smiled.

Traci looked into Raven's eyes and a wave of terror overwhelmed her. Her heart pounded in her chest. *This bitch's eyes are GLOWING! What the fuck?"*

Keeping her hand over Traci's mouth, Raven used her larger frame to pin Traci to the ground. She straightened out her body and lay on top of her victim. The pressure she applied to Traci's mouth with her hand made it impossible for Traci to move her head or neck. Raven ripped open Traci's pants and tore her panties off.

The fuck is this crazy bitch gonna do to me? Traci thought, in panic. *No, No, No! Please don't do this to me! PLEASE! Stop! Stop! Too much! Sto—Stop! AHHH! It hurts so bad! GOD! PLEASE! Make her stop! AHHH! Please don't push it in anymore! It hurts . . . It hurts! AHHH! GOD, it hurts! No! She tearing me, I can feel . . . from inside . . . AHHH! Please stop! Pain, Oh GOD, GOD! AHHH!"*

Raven looked into Traci's glazing eyes and watched Traci's tears flow down her face as the agony increased exponentially. "This," she said, "is what you were going to do to me, is it not? At least I didn't use your knife." She leaned down to whisper into Traci's ear. "No one can hear your screams, but I can feel your pain. Your blood is so warm. With every heartbeat, it pours out of your body. Can you feel my hand closing inside you? I'm going to rip you apart from the inside. Now you can let your friends know where you are." Simultaneously Raven removed her hand from Traci's mouth and yanked her arm out from between her legs.

"AHHHHHHH!" Traci screamed.

STARTLED, Ruben, Barbara, and Princey froze in place.

"What the fuck was that?" Barbara asked, grabbing Ruben's arm.

"It sounded like somebody screamed!" Ruben answered. "It was one of the girls!"

The three all turned around and ran in the direction of the scream, with Ruben leading the way, his gun held out at arm's length. They stepped into the darkness of the woods to search for their two friends.

"Traci! Mya! Where are you!" Ruben shouted.

"Ruben, maybe they went back to the car," Barbara said.

"We would have seen them," he replied. "The car ain't that far away."

"It's dark out here," Barbara said. "How do you know? I can't see shit."

Princey grabbed Barbara by the arm. "Fuck that, Barbara. They ain't at the car. We have to find them and that bitch. Now, calm the fuck down. We have a fuckin' gun."

They continued walking in the woods, parallel to the road, searching for their friends.

Ruben held out his weapon. "Careful. I see something ahead of us." They moved forward.

"Stop!" He held up his forearm. "What the fuck! What the fuck is this? Is that . . . ?" His words trailed off.

"Shit!" Princey cursed. "The fuck is going on? Is that them on the ground?"

"Fuck!" Barbara screamed, cringing at the sight before them.

"The fuck happened to them," Ruben called out to no one. "Who the fuck did this?"

"I did," said a voice off to the side of them. "And yes, they are both very dead."

The three instantly turned toward the soft voice, but they saw nothing in the darkness.

"They came looking for me," the disembodied voice explained, "but I found them first. It didn't go very well for them, as you can see."

Ruben raised his weapon and fired in the voice's direction. The weapon's report echoed in the silence. The women jumped behind him.

"It's that bitch from the club," Ruben said. "Bitch, I'm gonna fuckin' kill you," he screamed. He fired again several times, in multiple directions.

"That toy will do you no good if you can't hit what you're firing at," the voice taunted.

"Come out, bitch!" Ruben demanded. "Let me see you, so I can blow your fuckin' head off."

"Now, what fun would that be?" The voice now came from behind the group. They all turned toward it. "You're frightening the ladies. I'm sure they know by now that you can't protect yourself, let alone them."

"Show yourself, bitch," Princey shouted. "There's three of us. Come out in the open and talk that shit!"

"Very well," the voice said. "After all, the odds are on your side. However, since you asked to play this most dangerous game, you need to understand that there is no turning back."

Something fell at Ruben's feet.

"What was that?" Barbara asked.

"My fuckin' car key," he replied. "That bitch just threw my damn keys at me. How the fuck did she get my damn keys? They were in my pocket!"

Barbara picked them up and put them in her pocket. "This bitch is fuckin' crazy. Let's get the fuck out of here." Her voice quivered.

"We ain't goin' nowhere until her ass is dead," Ruben exclaimed.

"Here I am."

Ruben looked up to see her hand raised in the dimly lit woods. He could barely make out a silhouette. He fired his weapon continuously as he ran toward her. "I got that bitch!" he shouted. "I shot that ho! I know I did!"

The three got to the spot. They looked down, but they saw Mya's body lying on the ground.

"The fuck is this?" Princey cried. "How the fuck did . . ." Her words trailed off as she looked at her dead friend.

"Ruben," Barbara said, falling to her knees, "that's Mya. How the fuck did she get down here?"

"How the fuck I know," he snapped. "That bitch is fuckin' with us!"

"Who the hell were you shooting at then?" Barbara asked.

"That bitch we came to kill. I saw her ass. I shot her," he insisted.

"We just saw our friends lying up there dead." Princey's voice trembled as she spoke. "How the hell Mya get down here?"

"I brought her here to join us, so you could all join her in death," the voice now said.

In the dim light, she stood thirty feet from the group. They all stared at her, frozen for an instant. Rage exploded in Ruben as he looked down at his dead friend lying on the ground. He charged at the woman, intending to kill. He fired his weapon, but all he heard was the clicking of the trigger. He threw down the gun and swung at the woman when he got in range to strike.

"Yeah," he yelled. "I got you now, bitch. I'm gonna beat your ass to death." He swung wide and wildly, like a madman, striking her on both sides of her face with full force. Her head knocked from side to side several times.

"Yeah, Ruben!" Princey cheered. "Kick that bitch ass! Kill her fuckin' ass!"

"Beat the shit out that bitch!" Barbara screamed. "Kill that crazy bitch, Ruben!"

Ruben began to tire. After several more blows, his breathing became labored, but he did not let up. He continued swinging and landing blows to the woman's face. With each swing, he felt the power of his punches wane, until he was left exhausted. He removed his hand from her throat and placed them on his knees as he bent over.

The object of his rage stood straight up in front of him. She had taken all he had to give. "Are you done, handsome?" she taunted. "Please tell me that's not all you have to give. Please, baby, I want more. Please give me more. That felt so good baby." She spoke in a seductive voice that only he could hear.

"The fuck . . . The fuck is you . . . No bitch could take . . ." he said between gasps of air, as the strength drained from his body due to his exertion.

"What the fuck is going on, Ruben?" Princey shouted. "Beat that bitch down! I wanna see her ass bleed."

"Hold the fuck up, Princey!" Ruben gasped back. "That bitch shoulda been on her fuckin' knees half dead by now."

"Ain't no bitch can take a ass whoopin' like that," said Barbara.

"Ruben, baby," the woman said. "I think your friends are starting to get worried. They are wondering why I'm still standing, and why you look like someone who can't get it up. Look at me, Ruben."

He complied with her request.

"Play time is over, baby." She grabbed him by the throat and threw him against the tree. Turning to Princey and Barbara, she said, "Please take note ladies."

The sound her fist made when it made contact with his chest echoed through the trees.

"Ahhh!" Ruben's eyes bulged and his high-pitched attempt at a scream shattered the silence of the woods.

"Yes, Ruben," the woman said. "What you are feeling is my hand pushing into your chest."

Princey and Barbara held tightly to each other and watched in horror as Ruben's body went limp.

"Here you are, ladies," the woman shouted. "I think your friend would want at least one of you to have this." She tossed his still-beating heart at their feet.

"What the fuck!" Princey screamed. She took off running for the road, leaving Barbara behind.

"Oh GOD!" Barbara cried. "What the fuck are you!" Warm liquid flowed down her legs.

"It's your turn to die now," the woman said. "I'll catch up to your friend in a bit. I'll tell her you said goodbye."

"No, no, no," Barbara screamed. "Please, God, don't hurt me. Please don't hurt me. I'm sorry, I'm sorry!" she begged, holding out her hands.

"No, my dear," the woman said, "I don't think you are sorry. You're going to die. Maybe not as grotesquely as your friend, but you are going to die nevertheless." The woman approached the horrified Barbara slowly.

"Your eyes . . . your eyes . . ." Barbara's words broke off.

"Yes, they are beautiful, aren't they? No one ever lives to tell of their magnificence, my dear, and you won't be the first." The woman closed her hand around Barbara's throat and lifted her to eye level. "Now, tell me: what is your friend's name? The one who left you here to die all alone."

"Prin . . . Prin . . . ah . . . ah . . . Princey."

The woman tightened her grip on Barbara's throat. Barbara kicked her legs, in search of the ground.

"It's all right, child," the woman said. "Death will soon come for you. I just want to savor the moment and watch as the life drains from your eyes. Just as you wanted to watch as your friend tried to beat me to death. Unfortunately for him, he never had a chance in hell of accomplishing that. Here it comes, dear. Your body is about to shut down. Your brain is at the point of no return, as you slowly suffocate. Your last few seconds of life are upon you now. I can feel the muscles in your neck straining, the arteries bulging, your blood screaming for the oxygen, which I'm denying it. Don't fight it any longer. Give in and let death take you."

Barbara's arms fell to her sides and her legs stopped moving. Raven dropped her to the ground and went in search of her companion.

KEEP RUNNING, I gotta just keep running, I gotta get away from that crazy bitch. Oh God, please help me get away. Princey thought, as she frantically tried to find her way to the car they had left on the side of the road.

"Prin—cey." A sing-song voice called to her from the darkness.

Shit! Who the fuck was that? How that bitch know my name! Shit! She after me now. Just keep running. I gotta find the car.

"Stop running, Princey," the voice sang again. "You'll only make things harder on yourself."

The voice now came from closer to her right. Princey looked in that direction and saw a shadow moving against a tree.

"Shit!" She bolted to her left, running as fast as she could.

"Do you feel it getting darker, Princey?" the voice taunted. "You're running in the wrong direction."

Shit! What the fuck just touched me? This bitch gonna kill me. She gonna kill me. Shit, I can't see shit! Princey continued running, all the while trying to dodge obstacles in the darkness.

"Fuck," she gasped. "I'm tired . . . I can't, I can't catch . . . catch . . . my breath. Gotta keep running or . . . or . . . I'm dead. That bitch gonna get me. Ahh! Where the fuck . . . Where the fuck . . ."

"Where did I come from?" asked the voice, now very close. "I've been with you this whole time, my dear. You just couldn't see me in the shadows. And yes, I am going to get you, but I'm going to do so much more than just get you, Princey. But, before we get started, I'll even let you catch your breath—for what it's worth. Now, you must promise that you won't run away again. I'm tired of chasing you, even though I don't get tired."

Princey looked at the woman, and a sharp stab of fear ran down her spine. *That bitch's eyes! That bitch's eyes look like yellow light . . . What the fuck did we do? What the fuck did we do!* Princey again took off running, but felt a sharp kick to her leg. She fell to the ground instantly.

"See," the woman shouted. "I tried to play nice with you, and you disobeyed me. I told you not to run!" She kicked Princey so hard Princey was flipped on her back. "Now you get to feel my wrath."

"Ahh!" Princey cried. "Oh God, it hurts so bad. Ahh! It hurts!" Tears fell uncontrollably down her face. She curled into a tight ball and guarded her left side.

"Does it really hurt that bad, baby girl?" the woman taunted.

"Yeah . . ." Princey mumbled. ". . . Please don't. Not anymore," she begged, sobbing.

"How soon we forget," the woman said. "Were you not just a little while ago shouting for your friend to 'make that bitch bleed'? Well, you are about to learn what pain is, your highness Princey. By the way, my name is not 'That Bitch.' It's Raven."

With Princey still in the fetal position, Raven picked her up and simultaneously went to a kneeling position, slamming Princey's left side onto her knee. She let Princey fall to the ground.

"Ahh! Ahh! Ahh!" Princey cried. "God . . . help . . . me. Hurts . . . Can't breathe . . ." she gasped.

"I'd imagine the pain must be excruciating," Raven commented, "since the left side of your rib cage is crushed. Roll on your right side. That might help alleviate some of your pain. Here, let me help you."

"Ahh! Please, no!" Princey screamed in agony as Raven turned her on her right side, picked her up, and slammed her body down against her knee again.

"Ahh! . . . Ahh . . ." Princey's shrill screams echoed through the trees, shattering the silence of the night.

"Now you have at least seven broken ribs," Raven stated, "and while I do enjoy the sound of your agony, we have to put a stop to that." She positioned Princey in a prone position.

Princey lay helpless as she watched Raven raise her closed fist above her chest. *Eyes, her eyes.*

"Now, I believe that, in wrestling, they call this a heart punch," Raven said.

Upon impact, Princey's chest appeared to cave in and blood erupted from her mouth.

Can't breathe, can't breathe . . . Too much pain . . . God. Help me die. The gurgling noises she made were horrific.

"Now," Raven continued, "I imagine you're finding it almost impossible to breathe. Your sternum is crushed. And, by the blood you're trying not to cough up, I'd say you'll be dead soon. Therefore, I don't see the point in inflicting any more damage on your body. However, I want you to know this before you die: There is no God for you to pray to nor to ask for forgiveness. You and your friends caused your own deaths the second you stepped into my world."

Raven stood and gracefully walked into the darkness.

3

RAVEN WALKED OUT of the dark forest, miles away from the bodies she'd left broken and exposed to the night. The cold night air embraced her as she walked alongside the road, with the silence and darkness her only companions.

There are others like you, but not like you, she thought. *That is what that intruder in my mind told me before I destroyed it. Others like me, but not . . . If that's true, then I must find them and destroy them. There can be no others like me. I have noticed, of late, that I rarely require sleep, although when I do sleep, powerful revelations come to me that expand my mind. Also, at night or in darkness, embraced by the shadows, I find I can travel great distances if I choose, and my prey cannot see me. It is in the shadows that I feel the intoxicating emergence of the power growing within me. I will master it and if there are others like me, I will find and destroy them all.*

She walked in darkness along the road. In the distance, she heard a vehicle approaching. Before the car's headlights made contact with her shrouded form, she stepped out of the darkness. As the vehicle drew closer, her black dress shimmered in the light.

The vehicle slowed as it approached the woman walking along the road. Red and blue strobing lights lit the night, revealing it to be a police car. It pulled in front of her and stopped. Two officers exited the vehicle.

The driver spoke. "You want to tell us why you're out walking along the road in the dead of night?"

"Interesting choice of words, officer. Is there any reason why I can't be out here? I enjoy the darkness."

"No need to be a smart-ass, young lady. Just answer my question."

"Officer, I've done nothing wrong, and I see no reason to answer any of your questions."

"Boone," the driver said, "look at her right hand." He pointed.

"Is that blood on your hand?" the second officer asked, putting his hand on his weapon.

She looked toward him. "Actually, Officer Baker, it is. The smell of blood is intoxicating, is it not?"

Surprised, he looked down at his name tag.

"Yes, I can read your name tag from where I'm standing. I had to dispose of several people who attempted to attack me tonight."

Both officers now had weapons drawn.

"Turn around and place both your hands on top of your head," Baker shouted. "Do it now!"

"You can't be serious," Raven said. "I defend myself against attack, and you would arrest me?"

"Bitch, put your goddamn hands on top of your fucking head!" Officer Boone commanded.

She didn't flinch, and held her ground. "Tell me, Officer Boone. Did you and your nervous partner find those two bottom feeders I left sprawled in the middle of the road miles from here?" She asked with a smile.

Both officers moved to flank her position.

"Baker," Boone said, "call this in while I hold her black ass here."

"We should prone her out and cuff her first," Baker suggested, his voice unsteady.

"Do what I said, damnit!" Boone yelled. "I'm gonna have me some fun first."

"Neither one of you is going to touch me," Raven said, "but I can't wait to get my hands on the both of you. I promise it won't be enjoyable, Officer Boone. I just disposed of several lowlifes, and I would love to add you two to my kills tonight."

"The hell with this! Baker, cover me," Boone ordered, and holstered his weapon.

"Come," Raven goaded. "Please do make your attempt, you foolish old man. I'll show you who has the power here."

Officer Boone drew and snapped open his twenty-six-inch metal baton. He approached her with his weapon cocked over his right shoulder and his free hand in front of him.

She watched nonchalantly as he approached her. "Come Officer Boone," she taunted. "You're almost in striking distance. I'll let you come closer."

"All right," he replied. "You wanna play games? There ain't nobody with video cell phones out here. I'm gonna split your fuckin' skull for you."

Raven calmly faced him, her hands at her sides. He moved in to grab her left arm. With blinding speed, she used her left hand to take hold of his outstretched wrist and snapped it. The officer screamed in agony and swung his baton at her face. She dodged his clumsy attack, letting the momentum of his missed swing carry him forward. She caught the metal rod in her right hand and snatched it away from him, while simultaneously wrapping her free arm around his throat.

"What the fuck!" Baker shouted in awe and fear, as he drew his weapon and pointed it in their direction.

"Ahhh! Goddamnit," Boone cried. "This black bitch broke my fuckin' wrist! Shoot her black ass!"

Baker yelled, "Let him go now or I'll—!"

She cut him off. "Or you'll do what, Officer Baker? Shoot me? I doubt it. I have his big, bloated body between us. Are you that good a shot? I can see your hands trembling from here. So, go ahead. Shoot. I'm going to kill him anyway—and, trust me, a bullet would be merciful. You should have called for backup." She laughed.

"I said let him go or I'll shoot!" Baker took a step closer. *What the fuck do I do? What the fuck do I do? I didn't get a chance to call it in. She moved too fast. I didn't see. I can't take the shot with Sarge in front of her. I'll hit him.*

"Indecisive are we, Officer Baker? Let me give you a little incentive." Never taking her eyes off the frightened officer, she stuffed the metal baton inside his partner's gun belt and forced his right arm behind his back, holding it at the elbow.

"Ahhh!" Boone shouted in pain. "What are you doing? Let go of my fuckin' arm!"

"Baker," she called out to him. "Your partner... he's what, about six feet two, two-hundred-sixty pounds of bulging fat? Watch his feet." She lifted him two feet off the ground, holding him by his neck and arm. His legs kicked in the air.

"Ahhh," Boone screamed, "Put me down! Put me... Ahhh..." He cried out again. "My arm... don't... my arm... Ahhh!"

The sound of his partner's scream was unbearable, as the sickening sound of Boone's snapped arm reached Baker's ears. Baker fired his weapon multiple times to the left and right of Raven's feet. Dirt erupted into the air with each shot, and the weapon's report echoed through the trees. Baker's entire body quivered as he watched her effortlessly hold his partner's massive body off the ground.

"Is that the best you can do, Officer Baker?" Raven inquired, continuing to taunt him. "Did they not teach you how to deal with situations like this at the academy?"

"Goddamnit, bitch! I said let him go now!" Baker yelled, his false bravado fading with each second.

"By now," Raven replied, "you must realize that I'm neither afraid of you nor your little weapon. I may have to induce unconsciousness in your useless partner. I'll choke him out to silence him. He screams like a frightened little white girl. As much fun as this is, I am, however, growing tired of playing with you both. So, let's end this, shall we?"

"Put me... Put me down," Boone gasped. "I'm gonna fucking kill you... Ahhh!" Tears streaked down his face and piss down his legs.

Raven lowered him to the ground. Still holding him up by his neck, she pulled out the baton she'd shoved into his belt. She called out again to Baker. "I'm going to give you a chance to save your partner, Officer Baker. All you have to do is walk toward us. You can keep your weapon trained at his face. Come to me, and I'll release him. I want us to play a little now."

Baker could barely see her eye over his partner's shoulder as she held him up between them. His arms were fatigued from holding out his weapon and the death grip he had on it.

"Shoot her," Boone commanded. "I don't care... shoot this bitch now!" His voice was weak with pain.

"No one is coming to save you, Officer Baker," Raven said. "You are both dead men, unless you do exactly what I tell you."

What the fuck is happening here? Baker thought. *No backup. What the fuck is she? I'm not going anywhere near her. Whatever she is, this bitch can't be bulletproof. But if I take the shot and miss, I'll shoot Boone in the head. I can't do that. I can't take the goddamn shot!*

"Don't you move," Baker called out. "I'll shoot! Let him go now, I said!" His heart raced with fear.

"I heard you the first time," Raven said. "And it's gotten you the same result, so please don't make that request again. I will release him when I choose to do so. I will say this for you, Officer Baker. You aren't much of a partner—or a police officer—to let your man suffer like this. Why won't you come rescue him? He's out on his feet, and the only thing holding him up is me. That is, after all, in your job description, is it not? Saving those that need saving? But, of late, it seems that all the police can do is abuse the power they've been given. There have been many stories of late where the police have committed excessive acts of violence against black men all over this country. Do you have an explanation for this, Officer Baker? How does it feel to have the tables turned on you? In this case, it's a lone black woman, miles away from nowhere, in the dead of the night, that's torturing your partner, and you don't have it in you to do anything about it. Can you explain your own cowardice? Because I can smell your fear."

Anger rose in Baker, as he listened to her insults. A new resolve took hold of his mind and body. *I know exactly what this is! Something as ancient as man himself. It's the overwhelming need to either flee from danger or stand and fight.* His breathing was now steady and heavier. His vision was sharpened, and he felt his own inner weakness fade.

"That's it, Officer Coward," Raven taunted. "Officer Cowering, Officer Inept. Let it make you rush into my hands so that I may give you the death you deserve."

"Bitch, you are dead!" Baker took a step toward her and the baton she held raised toward him.

"So," she said, smiling, "you have found some hidden pocket of reserve bravery hidden in that weak mind of yours. Let's see if it remains after I put this baton where it belongs." With lightning speed, she lifted his partner off the ground and, in one motion, shoved the entire metal rod up his rectum.

The sight of his impaled partner was beyond belief. In his fright, Baker dropped his weapon to the ground. His mouth gaped open in horror.

"Ahhh . . . Ahhh . . . Ahhh!" Boone screamed.

Raven held him off the ground, and his screams got louder and louder. Blood poured out of his pant legs in torrents. She threw his massive body head-first into the back windshield of the police cruiser.

"Boone!" Baker screamed.

The sound of the impact of Boone's head upon contact with the thick windshield was sickening. Boone's shoulders came to rest on the back seat, his legs and arms spraddled on the vehicle's trunk.

Officer Baker stood trembling as he gaped at his partner's dead body on the cruiser. Too terrified to run, he pissed himself as he stood frozen in place.

Raven's hand closed around his throat. She forced him to walk backward until his back was against a tree. She held him by the throat and pressed her body against his. Even in his shock, he was amazed at the power of her grip.

"Now it's our turn to play," she said. "By the way, you may call me Raven. What would you like to do first?"

"Please don't kill me," he pleaded. "Please don't kill me. I have a family." Tears ran down his face.

"I'm afraid that's not an option," she said, shaking her head. "You are going to die, but first let me remove these thick cumbersome belts from around your waist." In a seductive voice, she said, "Brace yourself, baby. This is going to hurt."

She simultaneously ripped away both thick leather belts from around his waist with such force that he felt his pelvis crack. He screamed at the tearing of his flesh. His pants fell to his ankles and his hands found her body as he tried to push against the tree at his back. He was pinned in place. Tears now raced down his face. Her hands rested against his chest.

"Ahhh . . . Ahhh . . . Please don't . . . Have family. Don't kill me," he begged.

"You have a family?" Raven said, "How nice. I wish they were here with you. I'd slaughter them as well." She laughed. "You cannot invoke sympathy by voicing concerns for your family. How many of those that you have apprehended tried that same tactic, Officer Baker? How many black men have you shown mercy to? I probably wouldn't be wrong if I said none. I'm going to show you how that feels. Except, in your case, you know death is a certainty, only seconds away." She glanced down. "Officer, why are your hands on my waist? Does my body feel good to the touch? I don't like to be touched. Are you trying to gain some arousal before you die?" She looked down at his exposed underwear. "Tsk. How naughty of you. I can feel your penis getting hard, even as you stare death in the face. It is exciting, isn't it? You know death is coming, and yet you find it stimulating enough to get an erection. The pleasure I get from killing is so far beyond physical arousal it's beyond your comprehension." She smiled. "However, I do not tolerate being touched for anyone's pleasure. To touch me invites death. To feel your erection against my body enrages me. Did I give you permission to touch me in this manner? Will your little penis to go soft? If not, I'll tear it from your body and feed it to you. Remove your hands or I'll separate them from your arms."

He let his trembling hands fall away.

"That's a good boy," she said.

"You don't have to do this, I'm begging—"

"Stop!" she said. "It only makes me want to kill you more." She threw him to the ground and looked up. "This tree will do nicely," she said. "It's time to listen to you scream."

She took hold of his left leg and pulled him against the tree. She picked up his other leg, took one step backward, and held him there.

With the tree between his raised leg and his back on the ground, he tried with all his remaining strength to pull away, to no avail.

"Your life is almost over, Officer Baker," she said. "Don't fight it. I just want you to sing for me.

"Ahhh . . . Ahhh . . . GOD . . . ! Ahhh . . . ! His screams grew impossibly louder and louder as she increased the force with which she pulled on his legs. Raven pulled on his legs until his buttocks were off the ground. The sound of his agony echoed in the distance.

"That's what I want," she cried. "Scream louder for me! Sing your agony to the night."

"Ahhh . . . Ahhh . . . ! Officer Baker screamed louder, as he felt the femurs of both legs dislocate from their iliums. His mind registered nothing but intense agony. His gargled screams were mixed with his own blood and vomit, as the fluids poured from his mouth and nose.

Raven took another step backward and pulled harder. "Can you look at me, Officer Baker? It's time to make a wish before I rip off your legs."

The dying man's head involuntarily fell to his left side. The last thing he saw was his leg pulled from his body and the spray of blood through the air. What remained of his legless body fell to the ground. His blood flowed at the base of the tree.

Raven turned and casually tossed the dismembered limbs in the woods and disappeared into the night.

4

"THE GREAT MAN himself. Doctor Paul Laden. One of America's foremost surgeons and researchers. The one man on the planet who was going to solve every medical mystery known to mankind by experimenting on me. It seems our positions are now reversed. You were going to accomplish all that using the junk in this lab you call advanced medical research equipment; I've arranged for us not to be disturbed. I can tell by the look in your eyes how terrified you are. It's a helpless feeling being strapped to a table, naked, and not knowing what's going to happen next.

"Doctor, you have earned an exquisite, excruciating death. There was a time when I would have ripped you limb from limb, slowly, and agonizingly. Our methods have changed greatly over the centuries, so I'll spare you the unsophisticated tortures of old. Here, I'll cover your naked body. I'll at least grant you that much dignity. I'll even remove the straps holding you down. Now you are free to leave anytime you like, if you can.

He's really going to let me walk out of here, Dr. Laden thought. *I need to get help. I have to get away from him before he kills me. Wait, I can't move my arms or legs. What has he done to me?*

"Since you haven't gotten up and walked out, I'll interpret that to mean you wish to stay with me. Oh, by the way, I hope you don't mind me wearing your scrubs and lab coat. There is a reason you can't move now, doctor. After I rendered you temporarily unconscious, I injected you with a paralytic that specifically blocks all nerve inputs to your limbs. It leaves you unable to move but does not affect any other system in your body. Since we are going to be spending a little time together, I also took the liberty of halting your body's production of waste. Bathroom breaks will just get in the way of our discussions.

What in God's name is he talking about? He's insane, but I can't move.

Now, doctor—and I use that term loosely—while you lie there, I want you to consider this: I felt everything you did to me. Every cut, every incision, and the removal of every organ you took from my body. What you did to me is incomprehensible. You are supposed to heal patients, not butcher them. If only you had helped me instead of trying to exploit the situation, you would have been rewarded beyond your wildest dreams. Nothing you could imagine would have been beyond your reach. I know you don't care about money—but knowledge! In that regard, you would have been wealthy beyond anything you could imagine. What I find even more appalling are the motives for your barbarism: wealth, money, and power. You Homos never change, you never learn, and you can't see beyond your own ignorance. No matter your level of understanding, you can't help reverting back to what kept you in caves for millennia. Now, I'm sure you're asking yourself, 'What is he ranting about?' You will learn soon enough. By the way, doctor, don't you have anything to say? You may speak.

I can't open my mouth, how . . . what did he do to me?

"Nothing to say? No matter. I will tell you this, though. I will let you live long enough for us to have a profound discussion. How profound depends on you. You consider yourself a man of science, a seeker of knowledge, an explorer on a quest for the ultimate answers. I intend to provide you with some of those answers. Because science is all about seeking the truth, you will have the answers to the questions you sought. Unfortunately, this kind of knowledge comes with a terrible price. You will never be able to use anything you learn here today. But, what the hell. For however long it lasts, you will be the most enlightened Homo living on the planet. I will answer the many questions that must be forming in that twisted mind of yours."

He walked away from the table as he spoke. "So, I propose that we play a life-and-death game of twenty questions to test your so-called intelligence here today. I will allow you to ask me twenty questions, which I will truthfully answer. Now, there are rules to the game. You can't ask yes or no questions. I want you to have the answers you seek, knowing that the knowledge you gain will do you no good. You can't ask that I spare your life, or for any actions on my part to spare you the pain you've earned. You have five minutes from the time I answer a question to ask your next question. Your cost for a question will be to sacrifice a digit to be taken at a time of my choosing, so make the question worth the cost. You must start every question with my name. I hope you remembered it, because if you've forgotten it, the game is going to end quickly. And, finally, being a so-called man of science, a seeker of truth, you must continue until you have reached your twentieth question. The longer it takes me to answer, the longer you get to live. So, I suggest you formulate your questions wisely."

Where is he? Dr. Laden thought in a panic. *I hear him, but I can't see him. His voice sounds like it's coming from behind me. What have I done? Dear God, what have I done!* Doctor Laden was terrified. His heart pounded so hard he felt it might explode in his chest.

"Now," the man continued, "from this moment forward, I will refer to you only as Homo. You have no other name. You are no longer a doctor, a scientist, or whatever else you consider yourself to be. Failure to follow the rules or to answer my questions will result in the loss of a question and a penalty of my choosing.

"Now, for the most interesting part of the game. From this moment on, you will not see my face. If you do, it means you have failed, at which point you die horribly. If you last to ask your last question, I'll let you live. Your will to survive will be tested here, Homo, just as you tested mine. Now, before we begin, I'll give you the answer to one of the very first questions you posed before you started cutting me open. Yes, I was able to hear every word you spoke. Your question had been, 'Are there more like you?' Oh, I almost forgot. You can't move your mouth. I will restore your ability to speak."

Dr. Laden heard his captor's footfalls move away from the table and return. A mist sprayed over his face.

"Work your jaw muscles, Homo. You can now speak, but you can't move from the table.

What was that, a spray of mist? Something cool, liquid . . . the numbness is fading. I wasn't even aware my face was numb. I'm in my operating suite. I can't see the lab door. All the lights are out except for the surgical lights above me. On low intensity.

"Shall we begin? We call ourselves Proto Sapiens; we are the first and most advanced of the Hominid Species. As you now know, we have very special internal adaptations that set us apart from the rest of the hominids, and especially you Homo Sapiens. There are exactly fifty million of us.

"Our history began many millennia before your kind crawled out of their caves, where we had left you to your own devices. You measure your lifespans in decades, whereas ours are measured in centuries. While your kind had barely come down from the trees, we had already built great cities and civilizations across the world and fought devastating wars among ourselves. While we were aware of your kind, we saw you as our little hairy cousins and of no consequence. Barely more than apes. Not worthy of our attention, but we knew we would one day have a use for your kind. Many times, over the centuries, we almost destroyed ourselves. What we all share in common, though, are our violent tendencies, our warlike ways, hatreds, and the need to destroy everything around us. It was we who killed off all the other lessor hominid species, for sport or to take their territory. Then, one day, we came to realize that we had to nurture and protect your kind. It was a decision made out of necessity that we spared your kind, our closet relative. I'll get back to that later. Now, Homo, pose your first question."

"Damon, do all your people live in the Unites States?"

"We live all over the world. We control every governmental body on the planet. Millenia ago, we had adapted to every environment on the earth, from the freezing to the scorching. We have concealed cities in the jungles of our shared ancestral home of Africa and in South America; we have vast underground cities in the Saharan, Australian, Arabian, and Gobi deserts. Greenland, New Guinea, and Borneo serve as home to a quarter of our population. Our most spectacular city is in the middle of Antarctica. We also live alongside you Homos everywhere in the world.

"Do we not all look alike? What the outside world sees of the world and the locations I've told you about is what we allow it to see. Our technology is so far beyond what you have access to, it makes canceling ourselves child's play. We are in control of everything. For example, the famous—or the infamous—Area 51 of Nevada has always been one of our leading research facilities. Its purpose has nothing to do with the ridiculousness of alien life forms or UFOs. That was started as an experiment of hiding in plain sight to keep you people distracted. No Homo has ever set foot on that facility or anywhere near it, because only we know where it ends and begins. It is also where the first Artificial Intelligence was created. Contrary to popular belief, it is not controlled by the US government, military, or any other body save us."

Artificial Intelligence . . . What madness is he talking about? There is no such thing. AI only exists in movies. My lab equipment is on the cutting edge of medical technology. I better play along with him until I can get away from this lunatic.

Minutes passed in silence, before anything else was said. Finally, Dr. Laden asked, "Damon, how does the life cycle of your people work?"

"Interesting question, Homo—a question you might have found the answer to, had your experiments on me continued. First, in comparison to you Homos, our genetic structure is as close to perfection as it can come. We age like you, up to the age of eighteen. Up to that point, we are as vulnerable as you. After that, Proto time starts. From that point on, our lifespans are measured in centuries. For us, one-hundred-and-eighteen Proto means the youngster has lived a mere one-hundred-and-eighteen years. During those first eighteen years, we grow as physically large as we are going to get. Our bodies grow strong and healthy—many of us exceed your average height and weight standards, but not always. Our females don't sexually mature for purposes of giving birth until they reach Three Proto, or three-hundred-and-eighteen years. Our women produce no more than five children per century for five Proto. After that time, they can no longer conceive. So, every birth among my people is a true cause to celebrate; hence, the tradition of the birthday celebration. But I'll come back to that. Our children are always born healthy by our standards. We don't even consider the intervening years between centuries to be of any consequence because our lifespans are so long in contrast to your own.

After eighteen years, our Regenerative systems become active. Remember, Homo, those bio-nodes you discovered in my body? They are the reason we are what we are. They are our Bio-Chemical-Regenerative Glandular System. It takes 18 years from birth for these very special organs to mature. Physically, Proto males are easily five times stronger than the strongest Homo males. Our women are three times as strong. We can survive for months without food or water. In your mind, this may make us seem super-human. It's not, it's just how we evolved. Our children study for an entire century before they are allowed in the outside world unaccompanied. By this point, our young have earned several advanced degrees in multiple disciplines. We are a highly well-organized people. Many of us show no interest in interacting with Homos. For those of us that do, we have many Protocols we must follow. Now, you'll find this interesting. The oldest of us are over twenty-four Proto. No one of us has ever lived beyond Thirty Proto. We know our time is over when we feel our regenerative system shut down." His voice grew hostile.

"When that happens, in less than a century, we die. By your experiments, Homo, my Re-gen system was almost obliterated. And for all our knowledge, when our Re-gen system goes, we can't reverse it. So that you understand what you are dealing with, I'm eighteen Proto!"

Impossible! He's telling me he's one-thousand-eight-hundred-eighteen years old. Why am I not trembling? I've never been so frightened in my life. I'm scared out of my mind, but my body is not responding to how I'm feeling. Dear God in heaven, this whatever he is must be insane, and he's going to kill me? Help! Somebody please come to save me!

"Once more, Homo, I'll give you a brief history lesson about my kind to put into perspective what's about to happen. We learned millennia ago that our people shared a biological link that none of the other hominids carried. While we have a complete Re-gen system in our bodies, you Homos are born with only one of those precious organs. Unlike us, though, yours is active at birth. The organ you Homos have been led to believe served no purpose. Your appendix. If it were active, then Homos could fight off any invading virus or bacteria native to this planet that entered your bodies. It is the ultimate defense against invading pathogens. We have the same organ in exactly the same location. When we truly mastered biochemistry millennia ago, we couldn't have you immune to all pathogens, so we had to deactivate that most wonderous defense system in you Homos.

"So, thousands of years ago, we introduced a few confections into your diets: chocolate and beer first. Then we gave you tobacco. While those things can no longer harm us, we never touch the stuff. A few centuries later, the chemicals from those crude substances altered your bodies' biochemistry without compromising any of your normal systems. The result was a deactivated appendix, and it passed down as genetically inactive.

"Another fact you might find interesting: A woman's body is capable of extraordinary transformations—our women and, to a small degree, your women too. You have no idea of what a female body can produce. Your kind loves to speak of the miracle of childbirth, but women are capable of so much more. Something we refer to as Conversion. It's a truly wonderous process. I may tell you about it later. It's enough to know that we had to take this away from you too, since you people breed like insects. We have had to release all manner of plagues on you throughout the centuries to control your populations.

He is crazy. What am I going to do? Whatever he is, he's insane.

"It's time to take what you owe me, Homo. You have asked your first two questions. Now, I'm going to take what's owed me."

He's walking away from the table again. What's he doing? I can't hear him . . .

"You will find this very interesting, Homo." Damon walked to the end of the table and turned to face the doctor. In his hand, he held a beaker and stirred its contents. He uncovered the doctor's feet. "I'll just apply a little of this liquid to each of your big toes. Swab the entire toe. Yes, all the way around and we're done."

"Damon, what is that liquid, please?" The doctor lurched immediately.

"Ah, a question that almost turned into a request. Careful, Homo, that would have cost you. But I'll be happy to answer, although you should have held off asking what it is until this takes effect.

Oh, God what has he done. What has he done to me?

Damon moved to the side of the table and pushed a button on the side panel. The back of the table rose until the doctor could see his legs and feet. I want you to observe the effect while we speak. Watch carefully. . ."

My heart is racing, racing. What has he done to me?

"Ahh, Ahh!!! What have you done to my feet? What have you done to me!" The doctor screamed louder as he watched both big toes fall backward and stretch until they touched the metatarsal region of his foot.

Damon laughed out loud at the doctor's anguished screams.

"Ahh!" the doctor cried. "What did you do to me? What the hell did you do to me! I can't feel my feet. I can't move. This is impossible! What the fuck did you do?" He spoke out in torment, but with no expression on his face. When his screams stopped, he stared intently at his feet, now missing their big toes. *What the fuck? Why is my breathing so light? I'm totally calm, as if nothing happened. What the fuck is he doing to me? This is not fucking possible!*

"Homo, this is but a small sample of our mastery of the sciences. I can manipulate every system in your body using chemical, mechanical, or electronic means. I'll explain. But, first, are you done with your little tantrum? Are you in any way beginning to grasp the gravity of the situation you now find yourself in? I can't read your thoughts, but I know what you must be thinking, and it doesn't matter what the fuck you think! You pride yourself on being a practitioner of medicine. Is there anything in your experience that can explain what happened to your toes?"

Staring at his feet in disbelief, the doctor responded. "No."

"I don't have the time to explain thousands of years of history and scientific knowledge to you," Damon said, "but I will elaborate when necessary. Is your heart beating out of control?"

"No."

"Have you felt yourself perspiring?"

"No."

"Do you have any urges to relieve yourself of waste?"

"No."

"Do you feel any pain?"

"No."

"Do you feel what you would normally describe as fear?

"No."

"I have temporarily suppressed those feelings and urges in your body, Homo. Our bodies are chemical factories, as you well know. Our bodies are capable of producing all manner substances that enable us to survive. Our brains are far more complex than you know, Homo, and we have knowledge far beyond your kind. Using the crude substances in your lab, I have synthesized certain substances that, in effect, have shut down your ability to feel fear, pain, or anxiety, and that alter the cohesion of your skin and bones. I know it sounds like some shit out of science fiction, but can you argue with what your eyes are telling you? Unfortunately for you, when skin and bone are altered in this way, the effect is irreversible and those formerly functional appendages become useless. When I return your pain response . . . well, let's just say it will not be pleasant. In any event, we still have some time together, so pose your next question.

My God. "Damon, are all your people white?"

"Ha, ha, ha, ha, 'Are all your people white?' That's funny, Homo, but that question is to be expected from your kind. No, Homo. We come in the same shades of pigmentation that you do. We do not see each other as white, black, brown, red, or yellow. There are no niggers, spicks, Gooks, Redskins, hillbillies, gray boys, or white trash pieces of shit in our society. I think, for the most part, those disgusting terms cover all the races. We are all Protos. We know each other on sight, the way your kind recognizes its own. In all fairness, I must explain. The prejudices and hatreds so ingrained in your people are due to the way your kind has been conditioned by us over the centuries. I'll give you a minor history lesson; it would take decades to explain in detail.

"Many Millenia ago, on the order of fifty centuries, long before the recorded history your kind has been taught, the last of our great wars was in progress and we very nearly annihilated ourselves. My ancestors realized that, while we were the dominant species of the earth, if we kept killing ourselves, we'd be gone and you apes would inherit the planet.

"We couldn't allow that to happen, and we couldn't let our accomplishments be lost. In time and after much devastation, the fighting stopped, we erased our former past, and began anew. We formed ruling counsels among our people and adopted a course of action that would spare us from destruction and lead us on a course to becoming masters of this world. This is where you Homos played your role. The role we designed for you. Because you apes breed so quickly.

"A Homo female can produce many offspring in her short lifespan. Our females cannot. So, we needed a population that would serve our needs. To be builders guided by us, to be our surrogates in war. Unfortunately, the fighting continued among us for a time, but now it was your kind doing the killing, at our direction but always with a purpose. We would send to war whole populations, entire nations. We'd be behind every war to soothe our need for conflict. We'd play you Homos as if you were pieces on a chess board. But unlike chess, we played to attain goals you couldn't dream of. Remember I told you that you Homos only see what we want you to see? It goes much deeper than that. Everything you think you know about history, the sciences, the arts—it's false. Everything you've ever been taught in your schools is either half-truths, lies, or so full of enigmas no one will ever know the truth.

"We wrote your world histories and every event they all told. You believe that your recorded history began roughly five thousand years ago. It actually goes back much further. On the order of ten thousand years. Let's start with the mighty Egyptian Civilization. Every Egyptian city known to man and attributed to them was built by us twenty thousand years ago. My people built vast stone cities all over Africa and the world.

"We have always found stone structures to be magnificent and everlasting. We constructed those glorious cities with what you would today call modern building equipment. Our construction was indeed powered by the Nile, but not in the way you Homos have conjectured for centuries. We perfected the science of forging metal into tools and building heavy moving equipment long before we set out to build on grand scales. Our equipment was powered by convective liquid engines—a primitive technology, but one that didn't destroy the environment in which we lived.

"You Homos provided the labor for our projects, and you lived well alongside us, for a time. We raised breathtaking cities all over Africa. In time, we pursued other more pressing interests. After many more centuries passed, when we were ready to carry out our long-term plans, we allowed you Homos to move into what were our former lands and cities. Those who did so had no clue who'd built the structures, nor could they themselves duplicate what was all around them. We even created pictorial languages to go along with the cities you moved into, languages that you Homos would never understand. Even the famous Rosetta Stone has never truly been translated. We allow you to believe it's been cracked.

"Every major civilization of Northern Africa, The Middle East, Europe, Asia, from the Egyptians, Greeks, Assyrians, Romans: all of them were puppets acting by our design. We either directly ruled these civilizations or by proxy. Nothing that occurred in your history happened without us. We annihilated tens of thousands of you Homos with contempt. War was the easiest and quickest way to cull your fast-growing numbers. We instilled in you the very hatreds and prejudices that you carry to this today.

"We knew of every people in Africa long before we brought them all together, except for one. Most, if not all, were friendly, peaceful, and benevolent. There was one tribe on the southeast coast of Africa called the Ekon. They were a peaceful society of over twenty thousand. It was impressive at the time for a community of people to be that large. They were a well-developed, well-organized agricultural society, and they were more than they appeared. These people had never come into contact with us before. So, when we met, we told them of our plans for them and their lands. They didn't take too kindly to the idea. Not perceiving them to be any threat, we departed.

"When we returned, with our numbers two hundred strong, they were ready. Little did we know, the Ekon were fantastic warriors. Not wanting to outright slaughter them with our weapons, we engaged them on their level for the sheer joy of combat. They kicked our asses. Normal fuckin' Homos, or so we first thought, defeated us!"

The doctor looked at his missing toes and mumbled, "Too bad they're not around anymore."

"What was that, Homo? "Did you just say, 'Too bad they're not around anymore'? I think it's time to liquefy more of your appendages. You may protest without penalty."

The doctor watched as Damon applied the cold liquid.

"Now let's take out both number twos, and since you have earned a penalty, I'll get rid of number five on the left foot. Oh, by the way, Homo, you might be interested in knowing that this form of punishment is no longer acceptable among my people. I could face sanctions for doing this to a Homo. You see, normally, if given a reason to kill one of you, which is no problem at all, we'd either simply kill you in the primitive way you slaughter each other, or we'd simply erase your entire existence, including the family of a Homo brazen enough to attack one of us. Which would include erasing them, their family, friends, and all records that showed they ever existed."

The doctor abruptly looked up from his toes at Damon and back again.

"Now, Homo, let's watch this take effect."

"My God." The doctor began to cry. "Why . . . why must you do this to me?"

"You can stop with the tears, Homo. You didn't shed a single tear when you were cutting me open. I want you to watch as your number twos and five melt away." He walked past the doctor and stood in the darkness of the lab.

The doctor watched as more of his toes fell over behind his feet.

"I'm waiting, Homo. Pose your next questions."

"Damon, how did the Ekon defeat your people?"

"I'll tell you what we know, but that knowledge will do you no good. They defeated a small number of us in battle because we greatly underestimated them. They not only lived along the southern coast of Africa, but they were spread out along the entire west coast of the continent. How they escaped our notice is not entirely known to this day. We surmised long ago that, at the time of the great separation, another group of which we were not aware broke away from the Homo Sapiens tree: We Protos, the family that would become the Ekon, and you Homos. The biggest difference that we discovered between the Ekon and the Homos is that, physically, the Ekon were far superior to you Homos. They were faster, stronger, and smarter than your kind. If left to their own devices, they could have developed enough in a few centuries to pose a threat to us. The Ekon lived only slightly longer than your kind, on average about one-hundred-and-fifty years, and they had a marginally active BCRG system. They had an active immune response and one other characteristic that was endemic only to the

Ekon. As to how they defeated us, it was through superior hand-to-hand combat technique and chemistry. Along with their fighting skills, they also employed primitive chemical weapon technology. Our records indicate that their weaponry, shields, bodies, and their deadly hands were coated with paralytic agents that did not affect them but proved challenging even for us and catastrophic for all others. The exact details of the battle are not important, but when it was over, only a handful of our warriors survived."

"So, you can be killed," the doctor stated, staring at his feet.

"Yes, we can be killed, but as you are now aware, it takes a hell of a lot to kill one of us. Even though we suffered defeat at the hands of the Ekon, our elders at the time respected what we came to learn of them. So, instead of wiping out the entire race, we began to study them and their culture. No other people on the continent ever defeated the Ekon in battle. We sent tens of thousands of Homos to their deaths trying to conquer those essentially peaceful warriors, who only fought if attacked. We could have wiped them out in any number of ways, but we had to learn everything we could about them. After many decades, it was decided how they would be punished and what their future would be. After we wiped out their active immunity and weakened them genetically—which took centuries to accomplish by the way—we then set them on the course that they would play in our world."

"Interesting . . . How the hell am I not feeling excruciating pain?" the doctor mumbled.

"As I explained, I have suppressed your body's pain response for now. I heard you whisper that inquiry to yourself, Homo. All our senses are far superior to yours. We can hear even when we sleep. I'm waiting, Homo."

"Damon, how were the Ekon ultimately punished?"

"You'll find this answer fascinating, Homo. After the Ekon were altered, we allowed them to live in peace for centuries, but we never let them advance technologically beyond a certain point. In fact, we kept them living at a very primitive level, never advancing much beyond the farming communities they had established centuries ago. A trait we all share as a people, Homo, is that when one has all he needs, why look to change anything? That is what kept those magnificent people stagnant—that and our manipulations. In time, their knowledge of the chemistry used in battle and even their combat techniques were lost to time and forgotten, but not by us. So, after we established what would become the civilizations and cultures in Europe and let you Homos believe you were conquering the known world, the descendants of what were the proud Ekon race were ripe for the picking and would lead to centuries of their enslavement by your kind. Of all the Sapiens, only the Ekon were all dark-skinned. As I stated earlier, we Protos and you Homos come in a variety of shades and body types. All true Ekon males and females were dark-skinned, six feet or taller, and lean and muscular due to their way of life and training. The females trained until their bodies were magnificently beautiful. We took all that away from them and allowed you Homos to enslave their descendants for centuries all over the world and in North America. We also knew you would breed with those you enslaved, passing on your diseases and genetic defects and further eroding the magnificent people they once were.

"What would come to be known as the African slave trade you Homos engaged in for four hundred years was orchestrated by us when you were barely out of caves in comparison to us. The people your kind love to torment—the Blacks, African Americans, Niggers, and a dozen other crude names you use to describe them—they are all descended from the Ekon. Had your European ancestors faced true Ekon at any point in history prior to our encounter with them, they would have easily slaughtered you. That was the punishment of the Ekon for their defeat of us millennia ago."

They wiped out an entire race of people. Monstrous, absolutely evil. The doctor began to quake. He listened to the voice as it approached him from the front.

"I can read the look on your face, Homo. Don't feel bad for the Ekon. They got what they deserved. Take solace in knowing that, in a way, they are still with us, greatly diminished but still here. Oh, and don't think we spared your kind anything. We didn't. Your time for slaughter is fast approaching. You ever wonder, Homo, why deep down in the inner recesses of your mind you have always felt self-hatred? It's all right all you white Homos harbor that feeling, the xenophobia you feel, that inner sense of inferiority buried deep within. It's there because you are and have always been the lessor of the hominids. Your overwhelming need to strike out in fear: it's ingrained in your kind. That is our doing as well. We have destroyed countless species in this world, for one reason or another. We have also saved many others. This planet belongs to us. Now it's time to pay what you owe."

He's going to destroy more of my body. I can't stop him! Nothing I can do! All I can do is watch as my toes melt away. The doctor put his hands to his face. *GOD, SOMEONE WALK IN AND STOP HIM!* He watched in horror as another of his toes fell backward.

"I'm waiting."

When the doctor looked up, he was gone. "Damon, how advanced are your people?"

"Now that is an excellent question, Homo. It could take hours or even days to answer that, but since you don't have that kind of time, I will answer in as much detail as I think befits the question in the time we have. I will also allow you to converse with me, and any questions you ask on this topic will not carry a penalty. If we used the Kardashev scale—and, by the way, Nikolai is one of us, as were many of the greatest thinkers you Homos believed your race spawned—Homos would say they're at level six or seven. That is, of course, total bullshit. In actuality, you apes barely rate three point nine without us. Everything you have we have allowed you to have. Our technology and energy production are currently at eight point eight."

The doctor jerked his head toward the sound of the voice.

"Have you ever wondered who or what decides when the next great piece of technology or scientific breakthrough will be made available to the general public? Who is it that decides when ordinary people can have new tech? We decide. Take this lab of yours that you are so proud of. You think this equipment is on the cutting edge of twenty-first century medical technology? In my world, it's junk. Equipment we carry in our pockets and wear on our wrists has more computing power than all the computers you have in this lab combined. As an example, with just the cell phones we carry, I can access, destroy, re-program, copy, or permanently delete any programming on any computer you people have access to anywhere in the world, and you'd be clueless. Your computers are centuries out of date compared to ours. We control every satellite in orbit around the planet. We created the first primitive Artificial Intelligence centuries ago. We control what you do, what you learn, what you are allowed to produce, and how far you advance, and all at intervals we control. Now, understand this: we don't care about the ordinary lives of the average person in any society on the planet. You Homos are given fairly free rein to control your societies, with a push or nudge in the right direction from us. Remember: every government on the planet is either controlled directly by us or through our surrogates. The same goes for every major corporation on the planet. You are supposed to be a practitioner of the medical arts, and I phrase it that way because, compared to us, you're barely a step above a witch doctor. Take away your so-called modern medical equipment, sterile environment, drugs, computers, and assistants, and put you in an untamed, germ filled, uncontrolled wilderness, and all your medical knowledge is useless. I can cure any disease with what's around me or what I find in the field. We also possess true eidetic memories. We have knowledge of all branches of chemistry and the sciences that far exceeds that of any doctor or academic trained in your schools."

"How . . . How is that . . . ?" The doctor's voice was shaky.

"I told you that you may speak freely. How what?" Damon asked, with annoyance.

"How is that possible?" the doctor asked.

"Instead of answering that question," Damon responded, "look at your fucking feet and tell me if there is anything in all your training as a medical professional in your world that can explain how a chemical applied topically to the skin can do that to your toes?"

"No."

"It's possible because we control what you learn and how you learn at the highest levels of your society. In the beginning, we learned how nature worked and how to live in harmony with it. You are aware that many of the substances used in every field today come from our understanding of the natural world. Over the centuries, we created the sciences and mastered them. How many elements were you taught are on the periodic table?"

"118."

"No, there are six more not found on the tables you Homos study. Among other things, they give us the means to produce what you people call clean energy on a scale you couldn't imagine. Our societies are powered by energy produced through nuclear fusion. We let you produce electricity using coal, oil, natural gas, and primitive nuclear reactors. You now have begun to scratch the surface of the potential for using sources like wind, waves, solar, and even geothermal. The last four technologies, if applied correctly, could provide you apes with all the power you'd ever need. You Homos use dirty Uranium to power your nuclear reactors because we wanted you to. We had to eventually let you gain experience using primitive nuclear-powered systems. But if you had access to, say, Glitronium, you could produce clean energy with virtually no radioactive waste and no need to store radioactive fuel rods. Once again, the tech you use is guided by us, and because we can't have your inept use of technologies you barely understand destroying our environments, we have always neutralized the nuclear waste you apes have been producing, using another fantastic element you know nothing about: Merricium. We allowed you to believe that your nuclear waste is hazardous for decades or centuries and therefore a technology with a limited shelf life. You are taught that the carbon emissions from the burning of fossil fuels is creating a greenhouse effect that is destroying our atmosphere. Normally, that would be correct if left unchecked, except that we've fixed that problem as well. Every time an airliner or military jet flies above twenty thousand feet, the exhaust it emits scrubs the harmful emissions from the atmosphere."

"How is that possible?" The doctor sounded incredulous.

"The same way we clean up all your messes, Homo. Unlike you, we don't let loose anything we can't control or destroy. Since you apes need to fly, and we want you to, we created the jet fuel formula your dirty aircraft use to get off the ground. Inert chemicals added to the fuel activate when burned at high temperatures. As the exhaust is spewed into the upper atmosphere, the now active chemical compounds interact with the surrounding air to neutralize any harmful emissions. That is also why we are now guiding your kind to electric and zero emission vehicles. Believe me, Homo, we aren't going to let you apes foul the air we all have to breathe. Polar ice caps melting, sea levels rising, the arctic warming—that's all misinformation put out by us. We live in Antarctica. Do you think we'd allow you to harm that environment? Fuck no. It's all misdirection. In case you're wondering, we never fly on your aircraft. They are too easy to fall from the sky. On some occasions, we make them fall from the skies when we deem it necessary. While some of our aircraft might look like yours, ours operate on a different principle and we don't use liquid fuels."

"This is fascinating," the doctor responded. "How has all this been kept secret from the world? In this day and age, surely, all this would be impossible to hide."

"Ha ha ha ha! Homo, that is the very reason why the opposite is true. You refuse to believe that you are not the masters of your own fate or that white America is not in control of the world and all that occurs in it. I said when we need a distraction, we will crash one of your aircraft. That's true. The lives of Homos mean exactly shit to us, but it's nothing compared to all the wars you apes have fought. All of them were orchestrated by us when we needed you to be distracted. I'll cite a few examples for you. You are taught that when the so-called Pilgrims came to this country, they were greeted by the native people they encountered, and over time, the white settlers destroyed the native people. The natives they encountered were Protos. While they were peaceful and non-aggressive, they could have annihilated those they encountered with ease. That wasn't the plan, though. We needed your kind to eventually settle in North America, so you were taught to survive in a new environment and the Protos returned to their cities. Over time, some of those cities above ground were dismantled, and we moved to our subterranean dwellings, all the while watching and guiding you apes. Early skirmishes were staged for centuries, and we wrote the histories of those events and let you apes spread out across the country. Again, all this was guided by us. During every conflict in the US, up to and including WWI, we completed construction of our subterrestrial-maglev link. A system of hundreds of tunnels one thousand feet below the surface, connected from coast to coast, north and south, linking to what would become every major city in North America. We started WWII to launch spacecraft to the moon to begin construction of our base and orbit satellites that encompass the Earth-Moon system. Oh, and by the way, the nuclear bombs built and tested by you apes were done by my people. While all the nuclear powers of the world believe they are sitting on active nukes ready to go at a push of a button, they're not. All the world's nuclear arsenals are inactive. They can't be launched, activated, or tampered with unless we want it to happen. The same goes for your chemical and bio-weapons. Here is something else for you to contemplate. Every plague that has ever infected you Homos or decimated your populations, going back thousands of years, was our doing. We use these methods to cull your populations or, again, to create worldwide distractions. After we eradicated the Third Pandemic of 1855 in the early twentieth century, we decided that since you Homos were coming into the modern age, we should give you the means to cure yourselves, with our guidance if necessary. So, we instituted a program where every household in every developed nation from the nineteen-thirties onward would have the in-home chemical means needed to neutralize any infection. Since we didn't suffer from any viral or bacterial pathogens that could harm us, we'd give you the means to cure yourselves. After the many products that would be needed were introduced to your markets and distributed to become household staples, we decided that having the knowledge to use them in the way we intended was not necessary and could pose potentially dangerous unforeseen consequences. It was decided, by our ruling council, that it was enough that the ingredients were all in place.

"Why not share that kind of knowledge with the world you people created? The suffering that could have been prevented." The doctor sounded tired.

"We don't care about you Homos suffering, and as I said earlier, we don't unleash anything we can't control. Take COVID-19, its variants, and HIV, for instance. They are simple viruses that are easily cured, but they play a role in our plans. When the time is right, we will release the needed information to cure them. Isn't it ironic though that the means to do so now exists in every household in America? What's missing is the knowledge necessary to create the cures. We decided that giving you Homos that kind of knowledge and skill was not in our best interest. Your best scientist couldn't produce anything useful for curing the diseases that ravage you Homos from household chemicals because your knowledge of chemistry and biology is too limited and that's the way we want it.

"This is unbelievable! What proo—?" The doctor stopped and looked at his feet.

"You're learning, Homo. Before you ask me for proof of anything, just look at your feet. Here's a fun fact I'll volunteer. Have you ever wondered why there have always been two useless symbols on telephones that go all the way back to rotary models, or why hitting zero gets you the operator? Or why you people are assigned a social security number at birth?"

"No, I don't believe I've ever given it any thought." The doctor saw a figure sitting in the shadows to his left.

"The asterisk and the hashtag are used by my people to communicate over the telecommunication networks we gave you if the need arose. By combining those symbols, numbers, and the zero, we can call to each other anywhere in the world over your networks on secure lines. We can track any of you by using your social security numbers. When you talk on your landlines or cell phones, our computers listen to every word. Now you may have read this on the net: when you turn your cell phone off, no one can track its location. Most believe it, but it's not true. Our systems can find any cell phone anywhere, even if it's deactivated. We can listen through any cell phone or landline. If there is a computer, laptop, tablet, or gaming system anywhere that uses an operating system, even with a dead battery, we can find it and activate it without the owner knowing a thing. However, we rarely waste our time or resources listening to billions of bullshit conversations. There is a reason why over fifty percent of the world's population has a cell phone. Again, it's because we want it that way. You are aware that sound can kill, though we ended your research in that area long ago, with the exception of a few military applications that will go nowhere. We developed hyper-sonic weapons long ago that can kill any Homo simply by broadcasting a certain frequency over a cell phone or landline. The death looks like a heart attack brought on by a cerebral embolism. Also, the cell phones, computers, gaming systems, and Smart electronics you homos enjoy so much can be used by us to kill any of you we choose, when we choose, or to completely erase your memories by broadcasting pulsed-light and ultra-sound at certain frequencies. Hell the wildfires you homos fight each year we can douse from space. Many of them we set for our own purposes. Now that was an interesting conversation, but the time has come again, unless you have another question on this topic."

The doctor said nothing.

Damon stood at the end of the bed. "It's time to take away number four."

The doctor watched in horror as the last toe on his left foot disappeared from view. He looked at the remaining digits on his right foot and back to his left. The terror he felt increased with the knowledge that his torture and mutilation would continue. However, because of the unknown chemicals coursing through his body, he couldn't react with the normal feelings one would to the sight of his now toeless left foot. *What am I going to do? I have to find a way out of this or I'm going to die.*

"Next question, Homo."

"Damon, have any of your people ever broken away from your society to help ordinary mankind?

Damon stared at him from the shadows. "Over the many millennia of our shared existence, yes. Now, Homo, watch as number three on your right foot goes away."

The doctor could only watch as it happened.

Damon returned to the shadows. "Next question, Homo."

No detailed response this time, the doctor noted, *and no gloating. Maybe that question struck a nerve. Should I continue with this line of questioning? I only have two toes remaining, and then he moves to my hands. I'll take my chances with two more of the same kinds of questions. Maybe I'll learn something that can help me.*

"Damon, in what ways did your people help the Homos in the past?"

"Over the course of thousands of years, and before our awakening, some of the more stubborn of my people aided you by giving you primitive technology that you shouldn't have had. Helped your kind fight against us in battle, educated you in some of our ways. Thousands of years ago, some even attempted to start a new race of Proto/Homo hybrids. As a society, we considered it to be of no consequence and continued with our own plans. As I told you earlier, it is not forbidden for us to have sex with you Homos, as long as we don't produce offspring. Thousands of years ago, we discovered that Protos and Homos were sexually compatible; that is, the act of intercourse between us is the same. After all, we have the same sex organs, except ours are bigger." Damon laughed. "We also learned that while sex is possible between us and it is not forbidden for us to fuck Homos, there were startling consequences to offspring if they were produced. Now this will get a little complicated, Homo, so stay with me and the answer to your question will follow. Ordinary Homo sapien males cannot produce children with Proto females, but for those Homos, there are consequences for having sex with our females. You could say that an unfortunate male would become enthralled with her to the point she would have to kill him. Proto males can produce offspring with white-skinned Homo Sapien females, but the children produced are born with horrible birth defects. Proto males can, however, produce viable offspring with dark-skinned Homo Sapien females. Those children are not born with our Bio-chem system, but they live twice as long as normal Homos. "Remember the Ekon? It is believed that, somehow, they were introduced into our society long before we discovered and eventually destroyed them. There were certain factions among the ancient Protos that broke away from our earlier society. It may have been they who discovered the Ekon. It is believed that the Ekon were sexually compatible with Sapiens, but they never bred with them all those millennia ago. Not until their ancestors were brought to the Americas. By that time, they were no longer true Ekon. It is also believed that the Ekon were also compatible with us Protos. The offspring of a Proto male and a female Ekon was born with an active Bio-chem system and our physical strength, but without our longevity. These children were taken into our society to live as we lived, and they were instrumental in expanding our numbers. The offspring produced by a male Ekon and female Proto were always born female, and they were considered abominations. Recall that I touched on a biological process we call Conversion, which only occurs in the female body. It is a process by which the mother can manipulate the sex, mental abilities, and physical characteristics of her child in utero. We believe that these offspring somehow were genetically far different from either their Ekon or Proto parents.

"For those who chose to rebel against us those many centuries ago to venture out into the world to begin a new race of people, it didn't work out very well for them, as each faction was eventually hunted down and destroyed over the centuries when we got around to it. Nevertheless, it came at a great cost to our people. We were slow to destroy our own thinking that they would never accomplish their goals and could be integrated back into our society. Having learned from our past, we didn't want to revert to our old ways. We discovered, however, that it was a mistake. As it turned out, those traitors actually helped us. Genetic anomalies were passed down the line in the Homos, resulting in many of the genetic conditions you see today. Down Syndrome, Cystic Fibrosis, Huntington's, Sickle Cell, Hemophilia, Fragile X syndrome, and a host of other genetic conditions—all of which we can cure today, but choose not to. Helping you Homos develop was not part of our plans at that time.

"We did make use of what the traitors did for your kind, though. It provided the perfect opportunity for us to implant all the legends and myths into your societies that you still tell your children today—about monsters, demons, and all those things that go bump in the night. Many of those tales originated from the same source. The last Proto killed by a Proto wrote what is known the world over as the Holy Bible. A book full of fairy tales and nonsense. What's even more fascinating is that tome has done more to control and manipulate your societies than we could have imagined.

This is absolutely astonishing. There was something he said that I want to follow up on. The doctor watched as another of his toes went away.

"Next question, Homo."

"Damon, you said the offspring of a male Ekon and female Proto was considered an abomination. Why?"

"Deep in our past, when we thrived on violence, conquest, and slaughter, some among us speculated that certain factions of our people were led by women who were the children of male Ekon and female Protos, although this was never proven. Even we don't know the whole truth of these abominations, we only speculate. They were believed to be a hybrid of our races: neither truly Ekon nor Proto. Among their numbers, for reasons we don't fully understand to this day, it is said that some of these children developed certain abilities that set them far apart from the rest of us and that they were inherently violent upon reaching maturity. It is said that, in battle, they were feared among my people for their sheer ferocity. You see, Homo, our women have always fought by our sides in battle. Unlike your kind, our women are trained in all manner of mortal combat. The hybrid females surpassed even our men in their lust for blood and combat. It is said that they were nearly impossible to kill, brutal beyond belief, and only lived to destroy. It is said they developed abilities we could not combat, and it was those few who almost destroyed us all.

"Soon, they began taking control of our people all over the world. After enough of them had seized power and began to fight among themselves, they became known as the Dark Ones. They alone are responsible for wiping out uncounted millions across the planet. It is also believed that they, for reasons unknown, kept the Ekon concealed from us. It took many centuries, but we developed the means to eventually destroy those creatures. The last of the Dark Ones is believed to have fallen three millennia ago. Of course, much of what I just recounted is speculation because records of that time are fragmented."

Without saying another word, Damon walked to the foot of the bed, swabbed another toe, and retreated to the darkness of the room. "Next question, Homo."

"Damon, have you contacted your people yet?"

"I won't until our business is concluded, Homo. So, what do you think of my history lesson so far? You may answer that without penalty, while I take the last of your toes."

The doctor took in the sight of his toeless feet, and for many seconds said nothing.

"I'm waiting, Homo."

The doctor looked forward, past his feet, and stared into the darkness. "I don't believe I have the words to describe my thoughts at the moment," he said. "The things you have told me are without a doubt extraordinary. I believe you now. I'm just sorry I caused you such horrific pain. I betrayed my oath as a physician and a human being. I was wrong, and I am sorry for what I did—"

An angry, thundering voice cut him off. "Don't you dare try to feed me that bullshit! Like all you upright apes, you're only sorry for the atrocities you commit after you get caught! All you saw was the opportunity to exploit a helpless, broken patient. My broken form must have offered you the chance of a lifetime, when you saw my body's ability to heal. Remember, I heard every word you spoke while you were cutting me open. The one motivating factor that drove you, like all your kind, was greed. I say again: If you had done right by me when you had the opportunity, I would have rewarded you beyond your wildest dreams. There would have been no amount of money you couldn't have. I might have even expanded your medical knowledge to a point where you could have discovered cures for some of the many ailments your people suffer from. Yes, Homo, I could have given you all you wanted and more. Now, the only thing I have to offer you is death."

My feet are starting to darken. What's happening now? What have I done? Dear God, what have I done? I don't want to die. Tears fell from the doctor's eyes.

"Damon," the doctor asked, "if you came across one of those Dark Ones from your past and you had the opportunity to study it, wouldn't you? Wouldn't you want to know why they were as you have described them? Wouldn't you want to know what set them apart from your kind? I was driven by my need to know as a scientist, not just greed. I was driven to help all mankind by what I could learn from studying you. You are obviously a master of the sciences. Surely you can understand how powerful that drive can be. From one scientist to another: please, Damon, I'm begging you. Please don't kill me. Someone as advanced as you, you don't need to do this. Have mercy on me."

"I'll grant you this, Homo. That was clever, trying to appeal to the scientist in me. However, you are already dead, and the game is now over. You have forfeited the time you had left to live and your remaining questions. I didn't think you had it in you to see this to the end. Let us be clear: you are nothing like me, and the lives of Homos mean less than nothing to me. In comparison to what I am, you are little more than a prancing, savage, medicine man. You treated me like a lab rat, so now you get to have that same experience. The only mercy I will grant you now is the death you have earned. Before you die, Homo, you will tell me where you sent the organs you cut out of my body and give me the names of the patients you transfused with my blood. Then, I'm going to destroy this bullshit lab of yours and all the work you are so proud of. You will perish knowing that all you have accomplished has gotten you nowhere.

"Before you die, I will give you one last piece of information you might find interesting in the time you have remaining. Much of what I told you about my people's past is known only to our ruling council and the elders of my kind. The transplantation of Proto organs into the bodies of Homos is something that not even we thought to do. Among ourselves, there was never a need to even transfuse blood, so I must admit I'm curious to learn of the results of your experiments. Now where can I find that information?"

The doctor turned to his left and saw Damon standing there waiting. "All the data I gathered on you," the doctor said, "and on the transplant patients is on the main terminal in my office. The password is Laden, space, THE GREAT all caps, Three-point-One-Four-One-five-nine-star." He bowed his head, sobbing.

"Fucking disgusting." Damon snorted. "Interesting setup you have here, Homo. I can see why your people would be impressed with this lab. All this crap is ancient compared to our systems." He sat down and entered the password he was given.

So, he's held me captive here for weeks.

ONCE DAMON LOCATED the files he was interested in, he began to study the doctor's notes at an astounding speed, simultaneously studying the readouts on multiple monitors. *You have indeed been busy, Homo,* Damon thought. *What you have done is both madness and astounding. The council must be made aware of this, as there is no telling what the ramifications of these experiments will be. All three of the doctor's subjects survived the transplants, and one is known to have gone on a killing spree. These abominations must be tracked down and destroyed.* He used me to do this.

Damon looked around until he found what he was looking for. He ripped open the packaging on three new external terabyte flash drives and connected them to the doctor's computers. He typed in commands to download all the data concerning the Doe Transplant experiments. "The female transplant patient, could it be possible. What the fuck! I'm going to rip his fucking head off!"

WITH DELIBERATE SPEED, Damon rushed to the doctor's side and lifted him off the bed from behind by his head.

The doctor screamed in pain.

"I was going to slowly, mercilessly torture you to death," Damon told him. "But after learning what you've done to me, I don't have the time. I'm going to crush your fucking skull until your eyes pop out of your goddamned head."

"Ahhh! . . . Ahhh! . . . Ahhh! . . . *Pain, God the pain! . . . Crush*—The doctor went from screaming out his pain to making gurgling noises. Blood flowed freely from his ears, nose, and mouth, as Damon increased the pressure on his skull. The sound of his skull cracking under Damon's powerful hands was sickening. His eyes bled and bulged from his skull, teeth, and blood shot from his mouth like vomit. The cracking of his skull continued until his eyes hung out of their sockets and his body went limp and unmoving.

AFTER THE FILES HE wanted had been downloaded, Damon verified that all he needed had been copied and went about the lab from computer station to station, erasing all data concerning Laden's experiments. He went to Doctor Laden's office, activated his laptop, and logged on to the internet. He typed in multiple commands and was routed to the system he wanted. He waited a few seconds for the system to respond.

Verify . . . displayed, followed by a blinking cursor.

"Shit, I have to do this the old-fashioned way. No matter, once I do this, the council will know I'm alive."

He typed an extensive verification code and ended it with Proto Council Elder Damon, The Strategist of North America. The response he received was instantaneous.

Elder Damon confirmed. How do you want to proceed?

He typed: *Activate every computer at the laboratory of Paul Laden and destroy all data. Delete all data of my arrival at this medical facility. Do not interfere with the hospital's mainframe.*

Seconds later, with the exception of the laptop he was using, every computer, monitor, and medical device in the lab deactivated and powered down.

Task complete, appeared on the screen.

Damon typed *exit* on the laptop, and it powered down. He picked up the doctor's iPhone and dialed a number.

"Damon, where the fuck have you been!" said the voice on the other end. "I've been trying to contact you for weeks. I thought you were dead. Why are you calling me from an iPhone?"

"It's a long story," Damon said. "It is good to hear your voice again, Shango, my brother. We must convene the council. There are matters of grave importance we must discuss."

"You don't know how true that is. Much has happened in your absence these past few weeks."

"I'll be in South America tomorrow."

"I'll inform Ogun. I'll see you tomorrow, my brother."

After the call was ended, Damon stood and looked down at the now silent lab and the dead body on the table. He walked over to the closet and removed a clean pair of scrubs and a lab coat.

I need to get cleaned up and get the fuck out of here. He showered, got dressed, and walked to the lab's exit. He tried to turn the handle of the door, but it wouldn't budge.

"The power is out in this so-called lab. No matter."

He exerted force on the metal handle until he forced it to open. Once outside, he broke the locking bolt inside its housing that sealed the lab, and he walked away.

5

"EXCUSE ME. Could you direct me to the hotel's aquarium?" the stunning young visitor asked the woman working the front desk.

"Yes, ma'am. The entrance to the aquarium is at the back of the hotel, past the indoor pool. It's free to all hotel guests. When you get close, you'll see the signs that will direct you there." *Wow, she's pretty. I bet men kiss the ground she walks on.*

"Thank you," the guest replied and walked away. A few minutes later, she found her destination.

"Good afternoon, and welcome to Oceanus at The Ritz-Carlton, the largest indoor aquarium and attraction in Atlanta. Are you a guest of the hotels, ma'am?" the woman asked.

"Yes, I am."

"I'll need to scan your room key, and you'll be all set to explore the aquarium." She inserted the key into the reader.

"Thank you, Ms. Raven. You're all set have a wonderful time."

"Thank you."

Raven walked down a darkened passageway, paying no attention to the other people around her or the pre-recorded voice coming from the speakers overhead. The sound of flowing water and the cool blowing air relaxed her, as she continued until light could be seen at the end of the tunnel. Emerging from the tunnel, she found herself standing under thick glass and looking up at the sea creatures that swam above her. The large atrium had eight tunnels for visitors to explore. She saw the one she wanted, and proceeded toward it.

"They are magnificent creatures, aren't they? said the man standing next to her. "Although not as stunning as you."

"Was that meant to be a compliment?" she asked.

"It was," he replied. "I have always been fond of sharks. Of all the creatures in the sea, they are my favorite."

"Indeed," she replied, but otherwise ignored him.

"You know why I admire the shark above all the other sea creatures? It's not because of their size or power. It's because they are masters of their environments, and when they strike, it's without warning or compassion for those they devour. It's just the natural order of things. The shark has survived unchanged for millions of years because it's a successful predator and even evolution knows not to tamper with what works." He waited for her to reply.

"Interesting," she said. "I take it that you, in some small way, see in yourself the few admirable traits you admire in the shark. They don't have many."

"I'm not sure, but I think I've been insulted." His face registered disbelief.

"It was simply a statement," Raven said. "There is no need to read into it. And I can hear you. You don't need to stand any closer to me."

"May I ask: do you plan to be here long?" He looked up as a large Tiger shark swam overhead.

"My plans are my affair," she retorted. "I will be here until I'm ready to leave." She walked away to another section of the large exhibit, but he followed.

"Could you alter your plans to include having a drink with me?" he asked.

"For what purpose?" She kept her tone nonchalant.

"So that we can sit down and have a conversation. I find you very interesting."

"Perhaps. What is your name?"

"I'm Morgan Foster, president of Morgan Investment Group. And you are?"

"My name is Raven."

He extended his hand, and she took it. Her piercing eyes met his.

"Raven, when might I expect you for that drink?" He still held her hand.

"Don't. When I'm ready, I'll be at Neptune's Cove." She pulled her hand away.

"It's difficult to plan, when I have no idea when you'll arrive."

"That is not my concern. I've agreed to meet you for a drink. Now, if you'll excuse me, I desire to get back to what I was doing before you interrupted me." She walked away from him.

He looked on. *Beautiful she may be, but she needs to be taught a lesson on how to respond to powerful men and I'm just the man to teach her.*

Raven exited Oceanus and continued walking until she found her destination.

"Good evening, ma'am. Would you like to be seated at a table or at the bar?"

"The bar will do nicely, thank you."

"Please follow me." The host pointed the way.

"Tori, you see what Marcus just did? That was not cool at all," Karen said.

"Yeah," Tori said. "He seated her in front of all these people waiting."

"No, he damn near broke his neck to take care of her. Like he's gonna get some of that," Karen replied.

Tori laughed. "He may be one of the managers, but if one of us had done that same shit, he would'a jumped down our throats. I guess he thinks that'll score him some points with her. She looks way out of his league.

"Will this seat do, ma'am?"

"Yes, this will do nicely. Thank you," Raven replied.

"I'll send the bartender over. Enjoy your evening." He smiled at her and walked away.

"What can I get you, young lady?" asked the bartender.

"A glass of champagne."

"Any particular brand?"

"The best you have."

"Yes, ma'am. Coming right up." After a few seconds, he returned with a new bottle, showed her the label, and poured her drink.

"Enjoy. Just let me know if you want anything else."

She nodded to him.

Morgan Foster appeared by her side. "Well, I see you're finally here. I was beginning to think you weren't going to show. After making me wait for you for hours, will you join me at my table?"

"I don't take orders, Morgan, but you are free to sit here at the bar." She sipped from her glass.

"Raven, I'd prefer it if we sat at my table. We'd have much more privacy."

She turned toward him and spoke in a soft yet forceful voice. "What can you possibly say to me at a table you can't say here?"

He looked at her and sighed in frustration. "All right. I'll acquiesce this time, but you should know I'm not a man who likes to be kept waiting. What are you drinking?" He sounded irritated.

"Champagne is all I drink."

He sat down, summoned the bartender, and ordered a drink. "You're accustomed to having your way, aren't you, Raven?"

"As are you, Morgan." She smiled.

"Is that a smile on that beautiful face? I was beginning to think you didn't know how."

"I don't make it a habit, but not all smiles are meant to convey the same things."

"You are indeed a most fascinating woman, Raven, which is why I wanted to sit down and have a quiet conversation with you." He drank from his glass.

"To what end?"

"Well, we'll just have to see where it goes. Like you said, I am accustomed to getting my way."

She looked at him, turned toward the bartender, and held up her glass.

The bartender's response was immediate. He poured for her.

"Thank you."

"Can I get you another drink, sir?"

"Yes, thank you."

"Raven, what is it you do for a living?" Morgan asked.

"Whatever I want."

Clearly, her answer surprised him. "What does that mean?" he asked.

"It means exactly what it sounded like. I come and go as I please, and I do exactly whatever I want whenever I want. I am not tied to anyone or anything. I have all that I need, and so much more. You could say I'm a self-made woman. Did that answer your question? Quid Pro Quo."

"Not really, but I buy and sell companies. I finance some of the largest corporate construction projects in the country. I'm responsible for the employment of thousands of people. I'm also responsible for putting thousands out of work. It goes with the territory, when the weak and unproductive must make way for the strong and productive. I guess you could call me a Legion Partner." He smiled.

"Does it give you pleasure to destroy the lives and livelihoods of countless people in the pursuit of something as meaningless as money?"

"Meaningless? No, my dear. You don't understand. What I do has nothing to do with money. Although that comes with the territory. It's about acquiring the power to control one's own destiny and that of others. Great men seek the impossible challenges and do what is necessary to conquer them. They dare to do what lesser men can only dream about. I speak with CEOs of leading corporations daily. I can call senators to discuss business deals, or heads of state in other countries, including our own president. I've amassed a fortune and power beyond your wildest dreams, and all by the tender age of fifty-eight. That's how important I am, and if I chose to, there is nothing I couldn't do for you. But you would, of course, have to earn it." He smiled again.

"What a vain, egotistical man you are."

"Qualities that have served me well. Just as I'm sure your looks have served you," he countered.

"I need nothing from you, but it begs the question: Are you currently engaged in any impossible challenges now?" She drank from her glass.

"I'm sitting here with you, aren't I?"

She turned toward him when she spoke. "I find that insulting. It would be wise of you to choose your next words more carefully."

"I'm probably the most powerful man you'll ever meet. I think you should be flattered."

"Please explain."

"I have never seen a black woman in my life that I have found desirable, not even the prettiest ones in magazines or in movies. Frankly, I have never wanted to bed a black woman. You, however, are a truly beautiful woman who, for some reason, I find compelling. I look at you and I see the face of an angel. You walk with a grace I've never seen before, and you have exquisite taste in clothes. I always get what I want, and at this moment, I want you."

"Not a very compelling argument, but I will say this: I am not flattered in the least. I am not a thing to be conquered, and I have no desire to go to bed with you. In fact, I'll allow you to walk away and forget we ever had this so-called conversation. Believe me, it's in your best interests to do so."

He looked at her incredulously and put his hand on her thigh before he spoke. "I'm getting bored with this, and just so we're clear, you don't allow me to do anything. What? You don't like men? Are you gay or whatever they're calling it these days? I don't give a damn. Just name your price, so I can—"

"If you scream out, I will break every bone in your hand." She continued to drink from her glass.

"Humm! Ahhh!" He put his free hand over his mouth.

Raven summoned the bartender. "Why don't you pay for our drinks, Morgan," she said, "and then you can escort me to the aquatic gardens." She loosened her grip on his hand.

"Charge to my room: twenty-one-zero-six." His voice was stressed.

"Yes, sir. Have a good evening."

Raven and Morgan walked out of the bar holding hands.

"Please . . . let my . . . hand go," he begged.

"Not until we reach the elevator," she hissed. "Would your wife be in the room, by any chance? You smell of her cheap perfume."

"I don't know. Why?" He felt crushing pressure on his hand and his heart pounded in his chest.

"Well, if not, we'll just have to wait for her to return." Raven loosened her grip as they waited for the elevator.

"What does my wife have to do with this? Ahhh!" Pain shot through his hand and up his arm.

"Attempt to pull away from me again, and I'll break your arm." Her voice was calm.

The doors opened, and they stepped on.

"What the hell, how—" Morgan felt numbing pain shoot through his body as his back slammed against the far wall of the elevator. He crumpled to the floor, coughing and trying to catch his breath.

"On your feet!" Raven pinned him against the wall, with one hand around his throat, and pressed the twentieth floor button.

"What? How can you do this?" His fear was palpable. Sweat poured down his forehead.

"You have no idea what you started, Morgan. I was perfectly willing to allow your stupidity to go unpunished—until you touched me. You should never put your hands on another unless you wish to be touched back." Raven lowered him to the floor.

"Stop!" he begged. "I'll pay you anything you want."

"Anything, old man?" She looked into his eyes.

"Yes! Whatever you want! You don't have to do this—or whatever you're planning."

"I accept your offer," Raven said. "Lead the way."

The doors opened and Raven took him by his swollen hand.

"What are you going to do?" he whined. "Please, wait, you don't have to hurt me. Please, my wife doesn't need to be involved."

"I'm afraid it's too late now," Raven said. "I've accepted your offer. Is the shark now suddenly feeling fear? I thought you were the master of your environment. What happened to all that big bad talk you were spewing at the aquarium and bar? Tell me: what do you think is going to happen?"

His body trembled as they walked.

"I can smell your fear," Raven said, "and I can feel every nerve in your body firing with dread. Too frightened to speak. No matter. As I said earlier, your offer has been accepted, Morgan, and you'll soon find out."

"What offer?" he asked. "I made no offer. Look, I have large sums of cash in the room. You can take it."

Raven sighed. "You weren't listening. I told you money means less than nothing to me, and you're about to get a lesson in what real power is." They arrived at the room. "Looks like we're home, and the lady of the house is in. I can hear her breathing."

His eyes bulged as he looked at her.

She just smiled. "Open the door, Morgan."

They both stepped inside, and the door closed.

"You have a nice suite, Morgan. Is it a double?" Raven asked. "No matter. Please call your wife. We can wait for her over there. I'd like to meet her."

"Ahhh ...Please stop!"

She forced him to his knees. Excruciating pain coursed through his body.

"Touching me is what got you here, remember? Remove your unbroken hand from my wrist or I'll tear it from your arm." She increased the pressure on his hand until he screamed out.

A woman now came running down the corridor. "Morgan is that you!" The sight before her left her momentarily speechless and frozen in place: her husband on his knees crying, a tall woman standing over him smiling and holding his hand.

"What's going on here," she demanded. "Who the hell are you!" She glared into Raven's eyes.

"This master of his environment invited me here," Raven replied, "although not for the purpose he intended."

"Let him go and get the hell out of here before I call the police."

Morgan looked at his wife through tear-filled eyes.

"I see making threats runs in this family. The police can't help you now. No one can."

"Ahhh!" Morgan screamed, as the bones snapped in his hand.

"Now, Mrs. Foster," Raven began, "since it was your husband who insisted that I have a drink with him and since he agreed to forfeit both your lives, you can blame him for all that is about to transpire."

Raven released Morgan, and before his wife could react, Raven had her in a rear choke hold. "To your knees, Mrs. Foster, and pleased stop struggling. It'll only prolong your agony." She looked at Morgan. "I want you to witness this, Morgan. Remember what you said about the shark 'striking without warning or compassion for those it devours'? That described me perfectly. See, your wife is kicking her legs and struggling to break my grip on her throat because she can't breathe. Choking is an agonizing way to die. Now you will witness raw merciless power at work. Look at me, Morgan, and whatever you do, don't scream!"

Her eyes...

"Argh...!" *What the...! Oh God No?! No! Ahhh! Oh God what... What...!*

"Come now, Morgan. That wasn't so bad, was it? Believe me, she didn't feel much pain. Here. Take this as a token of her forever love for you."

His terrified eyes focused on the object Raven held in front of him.

"Oh, I'm sorry. You may speak, if you feel the need."

His heart pounded so hard he felt it would explode in his chest. Fountains of his wife's blood shot through the air. "Ahhh...! Ahhh...! Ahhh...!

"That won't do, Morgan. Your screaming might disturb your neighbors, and I need to shower and change. Unfortunately, you won't be joining me." Raven dropped his wife's bloodied head at his knees.

The sight of Raven covered in blood drove him insane, before she silenced his screams.

6

THE NIGHT AIR WAS calm on a tranquil evening in downtown Atlanta, Georgia. A stunning woman dressed in black strode into the Ritz-Carlton Hotel, walking with the grace and bearing of a queen. She made her way through the expansive hotel lobby, turning the heads of both guests and staff alike. All who saw her thought she had to be a celebrity of some type, or at the very least someone important. She entered a spacious, well decorated lounge on the ground level and took a seat at the nearly full bar.

"Good evening, ma'am. Can I pour you a drink?" the bartender respectfully asked.

"Yes, you may. Champagne."

"Any particular brand? We carry several."

"Dom Perignon."

"Ma'am, I'll need to get approval from the bar manager. We usually don't serve Dom by the glass."

"If you must." Her cold eyes met his.

"I'll be right back." He hurried away.

She reached into her purse and took out five new one-hundred-dollar bills and placed them on the bar. A few seconds later, the bar manager approached her, followed by the bartender.

As the bar manager got closer, he took note of the bills in front of her. "Good evening, ma'am," he said. "I'm Antonio, the bar manager. Diego informed me you'd like a glass of Dom Perignon. I believe we can accommodate your request. Dom by the glass is eighty dollars."

"That would be fine," she replied, and moved one of the notes toward him.

"Ma'am, are you a guest of the hotels?" he politely asked.

"I am."

"Very good. I shall return with your champagne. Diego, our finest champagne glass for the lady."

The manager left to retrieve the bottle. The bar patrons near her tried not to stare in her direction. Antonio returned, pushing a silver cart with the champagne in a chiller. He picked up her glass and held it to the light, before placing it in front of her. He opened the bottle, held it in front of her, and said, "Please, allow me."

"Please." She nodded toward her glass.

He poured her first glass. "Ma'am, would you be more comfortable at a booth? I have a private area that is very comfortable with a beautiful view." For a second, Antonio found himself almost mesmerized as he looked into her eyes.

"No thank you. I'm fine right here for a while."

"Will you be dining with us this evening?"

"Perhaps," she replied. "I haven't decided."

"May I ask your name?"

"It's Raven."

"Raven. She who is the beauty who walks in the night. It is from a poem I once read." He smiled, turned, and signaled for Diego. "Diego, please pour for Ms. Raven when she's ready, and let me know if she requires anything else."

"Yes, sir."

"It has been a pleasure meeting you, Raven." Antonio bowed slightly in her direction before leaving.

"Ma'am, would you like an appetizer?" Diego asked.

"No, Diego, and please call me Raven." She took a drink from her glass.

"All right, Raven. Let me know when you're ready for another glass." He left to wait on other patrons.

"That's a lot of champagne for one little lady."

Raven turned to the man sitting next to her.

"How about sharing and a little conversation?" he said. "I'm Carl, by the way."

"I'm not in a sharing mood," she replied, "and I don't desire a conversation." She drank from her glass.

"All right, just trying to be friendly."

She didn't respond to him.

He signaled for the bartender. "Diego, let me get another Jack and Coke."

"Yes, sir." Diego poured the drink into a fresh glass and put it in front of the customer.

"Raven, are you ready for another glass of champagne?" Diego asked.

"Yes, thank you."

He poured her drink, and she pushed a one-hundred-dollar bill toward him.

"Thank you, Raven." He took the bill.

"Raven. That's a pretty name. Are you here alone tonight?" Carl asked.

She ignored the question and drank from her glass.

"You don't have to be so cold," Carl said. "We're all at a bar to have a good time. A little conversation won't kill you." He placed his hand on her forearm.

She looked down at his hand and then into his eyes. "Remove your hand or I'll remove it from your arm. I will not ask you again to leave me alone." Her glare was menacing.

The look in her eyes gave him pause. He quickly removed his hand. "I'm sorry," he stammered. "I didn't mean any harm. I'll just go sit somewhere else." He picked up his drink and left.

The man seated next to Carl's now empty seat began to snicker. "I think you scared him off sister." He turned toward Raven. "Mind if I take that seat?"

Raven did not respond, so he took the empty seat.

"Hi, my name is—"

She cut him off. "I don't care what your name is. I have no desire to talk to you either."

"All right, cool. I'll leave you alone." *Fuck you then, bitch.* He returned to where he'd been seated.

"MAN, THAT PRETTY ASS ho shut me down. She must be a fuckin' dyke," Ronald said to his friend.

"She the finest motherfucker in this bar, and she knows it," his friend Fortune replied. "I told you. That bitch drinkin' shit that cost a hundred dollars a glass. That's way out of my league. You heard what she said to that old ass gray boy. Man, fuck her. There are plenty of single women out tonight." He laughed.

Raven finished her champagne and looked across the bar to signal the bartender, but she didn't see him. A few seconds later, Antonio walked up to her.

"Raven, a gentleman sitting at a private table would like to buy you a drink and asks that you join him."

"Antonio, you can tell whoever it is I do not respond to summonses, and I am perfectly capable of buying my own drinks."

"Very well. Can I pour you another?"

"Yes." She held up her glass.

Diego returned and began picking up the empty glasses around his section of the bar.

"Hey, Diego. Another Patron, please," a patron ordered.

He passed Raven and she stopped him. "Diego, I'll be back in a few moments," she said.

"No problem, Raven. I got you." He removed the expensive champagne glass and cash and replaced them with a marker to hold her seat open.

Raven walked to the bar's exit, and many of its patrons took notice. Raven walked out of the ladies' room and turned toward the entrance to the bar. As she got closer, she noticed a large man wearing a black suit and an earpiece standing outside the entrance. He walked toward her.

"Ma'am. Senator Porter requests that you join him at his table."

She quickly looked him up and down, and a slight smile formed on her face. "Why would I want to do that?"

He seemed puzzled at her response. "The senator would like to meet you."

"You can tell this person that I have no such desire. Now, if you will step aside, I'd like to get back to my seat."

When he didn't move, Raven started to walk around him. He touched his earpiece and put his arm out to stop her.

She looked up at him and their eyes met. "Do you intend to bar my way? I could easily move you myself," she said with disdain.

"Ma'am, please. Can you just follow me to the senator's table? This will not take up too much of your time."

She held her ground, a look of contempt in her eyes. "Very well, lead the way."

They walked down to the end of a dimly lit hallway and through a door that led to the bar's private suites. He led her up three flights of stairs. They walked down a corridor and stopped at the fifth door.

"Ma'am, what is your name so I can introduce you to the senator."

"Raven."

He opened the door and she followed him inside. "Please come this way." The large man instructed.

They walked into the private lounge and down four stairs. To the left, a fire was burning in a gas fireplace. A leather sofa was set against the back wall and a large flat-screen TV on the far-right wall. The TV was placed between two doors, and lounge chairs faced large one-way glass panels. From this vantage point, almost the entire bar and restaurant area could be seen through the glass.

"Ms. Raven, please have a seat. The senator will be out in a moment. Can I get you anything?"

"No." Raven sat on the sofa.

A door opened to the left of the large TV and a man emerged.

"Senator Porter, may I introduce Raven," said the man in the black suit. "Raven, this is Senator Porter."

The senator walked over to Raven with his hand extended. She stood and took the offered hand. "I'm pleased you accepted my invitation. Can I get you a drink, Raven?"

"Champagne."

"Let's sit at the bar."

"Senator, will you be needing anything else?" the man asked.

"No, Martin. Thank you. I believe I have what I want."

"Good evening, senator. Ms. Raven," Martin replied, and left the lounge through the door to the right of the big screen.

The senator placed a glass of champagne in front of Raven and sat at the bar next to her.

"You have interrupted my evening," Raven said, "so what is it that you want?"

"Why, just the company of one of the most stunning women I've ever seen," the senator replied.

"Is that supposed to flatter me?"

"It's the truth, but I'm sure you hear that all the time." He smiled.

"What is your name? I hope you don't expect me to call you 'Senator,' because that doesn't impress me either."

"My name is Nathan. Are you always this abrupt, Raven?"

"I am." She looked at the glass before she took a drink.

"Raven, I'd like you to have dinner with me this evening."

"I'm not hungry."

"In that case, how about some quiet conversation by the fire."

"Wouldn't your time be better spent with your wife? The tan line on your ring finger is obvious, even against your pale skin." She stood and walked to the large glass panel.

"My wife and I are what you might call free spirits," the senator said. "As long as we are discreet, we both are free to do as we please."

"So, tell me, Nathan," Raven said. "What is it you expect from me that would require discretion, other than my company?"

"I'm a very wealthy and powerful man. I was hoping we could be friends. Having someone like me on your side would make for a powerful ally." He got up and stood behind her, his body just inches away from hers. Looking down at her straight, shimmering, black hair, the smell of her perfume excited him.

"I am not looking to form an alliance," she retorted. "Your wealth and power mean nothing to me. And please back away from me."

"You are a very mysterious woman, Raven. I find it exhilarating." He moved back to the bar and took a drink from his glass.

She turned to face him. "How many women have you seduced in this way?"

"I'm a man who gets what he wants."

"I take it you would like to add me as another of your conquests. How very disappointing." She walked toward him and held out her glass.

He filled it and was captivated by her eyes. "I wouldn't put it in those terms," he replied, feeling a bit deflated.

"This is a most dangerous game you're playing," she said. "You see yourself as the hunter, the stalker, and finally the conqueror, but how would you react if you found yourself in the role of the prey?" A seductive smile spread across her face.

"That's a role I'll never find myself in." He smiled again.

"And why is that, Nathan?"

He stood and looked her in the eye. "Because when you're the hunter, you're prepared to win. Every possible contingency is laid out; every move is planned for and countered. No escape, no exits. That's how you run a business—and a Senate committee. When you wield power, you have control, and control is everything."

Raven responded, her voice now seductive, her smile sinister. "But what if you found yourself hunting something unknown to you? Something you've never encountered before. Would you know how to make the proper adjustments necessary to take down the prey? Or would you find yourself hoping that what worked in the past would somehow pull you out of the fire you now find yourself in?"

"That's an interesting conundrum, but how does that apply to me?"

She moved close to him. "Because I'm in the role of the hunter now."

"Ha ha ha ha! You are an intriguing woman Raven. But I have to tell you, I'll never be anyone's prey." He sat in a bar chair and drank from his glass.

"Oh, but you are now, Nathan," she whispered.

The look in her eyes startled him for a second as she walked past him.

"Do not move from that seat, Nathan," she said.

What the fuck? Why can't I move?

"You should have never called me up here," Raven continued. "I was content to savor my champagne in the relative peace of the bar. You gave me a drink spiked with poison. What is it? X, or some other concoction you've used in the past? I knew it the moment you poured my drink. Since I knew it wouldn't affect me, I played along with your little charade. Now I am hungry, Nathan, but not for food. Are you wondering why it's so difficult for you to stand? It's what you might call my 'perfume.' I want you to savor the fragrance." She stood in front of him and placed her hands on his shoulders. "Look at me, Nathan. Please tell me now why you brought me up here, and please be honest." Her voice was seductive.

"We wanted to have sex with you," Nathan confessed. "I was hoping we could have a three-way. I would have paid you well. You are so beautiful. You wouldn't have been harmed."

"So, I'll assume when you say 'we,' you are referring to the idiot that escorted me here. Both of you planned to rape me, but I wouldn't have been harmed. That's one hell of an oxymoron."

He looked into her eyes, and he was terrified by what he saw. *What the fuck is wrong with her eyes? What is she? What is she doing to me? Martin! Martin! Get out here!*

"Is your man waiting for you to come get him?" Raven asked. "I know he's listened to every word we have said. I wonder why he hasn't come out of hiding. Does he like to watch you rape drugged women, and then he takes the leftovers? Or do you both fuck them at the same time?"

"Sometimes . . ." Nathan lowered his head.

The door opened, and Martin emerged. He had a gun drawn and pointed at Raven's head. His shirt was untucked and his tie was off. "Let him go now!" he commanded Raven.

"What are you talking about?" Raven responded.

"I said let him go."

"I'm not holding him. We were just having a quiet and, I thought, private conversation." She put her arm around Nathan's shoulder.

"Don't make me shoot you, bitch. Move away from him! Now!"

"If you do that, Martin, the whole world is going to see you shoot an unarmed woman. You see my purse on the bar. There's a micro-camera pointing right at you, recording everything that's said and done in this room. It's sending video to my computer and internet account. I never leave home without it."

He looked at the bar and saw her handbag sitting upright on the bar. *Fuck! Goddamnit what the fuck!* Martin held his ground, not wanting to get any closer to her.

"Put away the gun and I'll take my bag and leave," she said in a playful tone.

"No," Martin yelled. "You get the fuck out of here, now!"

She quickly moved away from the senator and picked up the hotel phone on the bar. "You won't let me leave? Okay. I'll call the front desk and get security up here."

"Martin, holster the goddamned gun," the senator ordered, "and let her get her purse and get out of here."

"Senator, if we let her leave, she can bring both of us down." Martin put away the gun.

"No, Martin," Raven said. "I have no intention of 'bringing you both down.' You two wanted to play, so we'll play." She slowly walked toward him.

"Look, goddamnit, just leave and forget you ever came here." Martin took her by her left arm.

Before he could react, Raven gripped his right hand, placed the big man in a wrist lock, snapped his wrist, and took him to the floor with an armbar. He screamed as he was slammed to the floor.

"How does that feel, Martin?" she taunted.

"Ahhh! . . . Let go!" he screamed.

The action happened so fast the senator had no time to properly process what he saw.

"Is that all you have to say, Martin? How about I give you a reason to scream." Still in an armbar and with brutal force, she used her left hand to break his arm.

"Ahhh! . . . Ahhh!—"

"Stop whining." She lifted Martin off the floor by his shoulders and threw him onto the sofa. She removed his weapon and tossed it near the fireplace.

"What in the name . . ." The senator stood in awe at what he was witnessing.

"What . . . What the fuck! Ahhh! That bitch broke my fuckin' arm." Martin exclaimed in agony, guarding his right arm.

Raven turned to the senator, who sat frozen like a deer in headlights. "Now, Nathan, are you ready to play? And don't even think about going after that gun or I'll make it cum in your mouth."

"What in God's name are you? No women could do what you just did." Nathan's voice trembled.

"Let's just say I'm more than you bargained for, and leave it at that."

"Look, just leave." His voice was now filled with fear. He held his hands out in front of him.

"I'm not ready to leave just yet," Raven said. "I told you: you were playing a most dangerous game. Now you're going to find out just how dangerous, my prey."

She approached, and he stepped backward behind the bar.

"I hope you're not thinking of pulling a weapon on me, Nathan. It'll only make things worse." She stopped at the bar that stood between them.

"What is it you want?" he cried. "Do you want money? I'll pay you anything you want. Power? Through me, you can have that too. Just don't do anything rash." He tried to sound brave.

"I have power," Raven said, "but not in the way you mean. And I don't need your money, but since you offered it, how does one million dollars sound?"

"You must be insane. I'm not going to just hand over that kind of money."

"Your eyes betray you, Nathan." She walked over to Martin, who was trying to retrieve his weapon.

"Ahhh!" he screamed, as she kicked him in his side so hard he flipped over on his back. He felt some of his ribs break. "Ahhh!" he screamed again.

"Senator, run!" Martin yelled out in pain.

Raven got in front of Nathan before he could reach the door. She shoved him so hard he fell on his back, five feet from where he stood. The force of her blow left him gasping for air.

"'No escape, no exit.' Remember, Nathan?" She picked him up by his throat. Instantly both his hands clutched hers. She tightened her grip. He began to make gurgling sounds.

"Remove your hands, Nathan, or I'll snap your neck like a dried-out twig."

He did as he was told and was thrown into a lounge chair.

She went to her handbag and took out her cell phone and a card. "Now, my prey, you will transfer one million dollars into the account I'm going to give you, and we can consider the matter closed."

"You must be fucking insane, if you think I'm going to do that. Even if you kill me, you won't get away with this shit, you fucking lunatic. I'm a goddamn US Senator, you crazy bitch!"

"We will see, my prey. And those very ugly words are going to cost you dearly. Remember who invited whom up here. I'm going to enjoy this. Remove your clothes, Nathan."

The sight of her eyes terrified him. "I'm not," he said. "I'm not going to do a damn thing."

Raven smacked him so hard that blood flew from his mouth as he fell to the floor. She went to Martin, grabbed him by his shoulders, and threw him in front of the senator like a ragdoll. She tore off Martin's pants as if they were made of tissue. She tore off the senator's clothes in the same manner, and forced him to stand in front of his bodyguard. She stood behind the senator, holding him by the back of his neck.

"Please just let us go," Nathan pleaded. "You don't have to . . . you don't have to kill us. Please. I'm sorry." Tears fell down the senator's face. Both men quaked with fear.

"Yes, you are indeed my prey," Raven said, "and a sorry excuse for a human being. However, you are not as sorry as you're going to be. Your plan was for you and your dog to rape me. Let's see if after a few minutes of my game you are still so inclined. Dog, since you are already on your knees, suck the cock of my prey. Give it what I'm sure you wanted to take from me."

Martin looked up, averting his eyes from the quaking, naked man being forced to stand in front of him.

"Bitch, you may as well kill me now. You can go straight to hell." He spoke with defiant rage. He looked at her again, and a wave of terror flowed through his body. *Her fuckin' eyes! What the fuck is going on with her fuckin' eyes?*

"Do not utter another word, dog. Put your master's cock in your mouth or I'll tear off your head from your bloated body—very slowly."

Oh God, what the fuck is she? I can't stop myself from doing this shit. With tears falling down his face, Martin did as he was compelled to do.

"Now, dog, pleasure your master's cock. Let your eyes savor every moment, and perform like you know how. That's a good dog. Let it get hard in your mouth. Use your good hand to bring your master to climax. Take all your master has to give." Tears flowed down the faces of both men as they were forced to do the unthinkable.

Raven whispered in the senator's ear. "You thought you knew what power was, my prey? This is power. Open your eyes and look down at your dog as he performs the act that you so enjoyed taking from others. Let your eyes meet his. Enjoy the sight of your cock in his mouth. If I were you, I'd enjoy it in the time you have left to live, as it may soon be coming to an end. You have my permission to savor the experience, prey. While you do so, contemplate this: Make the transfer, and you and your dog may live to remember this experience for the rest of your lives. You'll never see me again. Or, there is the alternative. You both die here and now, horrendously. You have until your dog makes you cum to decide."

Raven took a seat in a lounge chair and watched as the senator brought his hands to his face, crying like a child while his confidant, bodyguard, and fellow rapist gave him head until he came.

"Dog, let your master spray on your face."

Martin cried out loud as cum squirted on his face and into his mouth. When Martin released Nathan's penis, the senator backed away, trembling and barely able to stand. He steadied himself using one of the barstools.

"Stay on your knees, dog," Raven commanded. "What will it be, my prey? Do you wish to continue living, or do you both die now?"

"Dear God. What did you make me do? Yes, okay! Okay! I'll give you the money." His voice trembled.

"A wise choice. Stay right where you are, and we can get this over with." Raven walked over to the sink and wet a towel.

"Wipe your hands, sit down, and we can finish this." She handed the senator her cell phone.

"Access an account your wife is oblivious to."

He looked at her in surprise.

She mocked him. "I'm sure one as powerful as you has several accounts his free-spirited wife knows nothing about."

After several seconds, he accessed the account he wanted and looked up at Raven.

She handed him a card with her account number.

"Is this an offshore account?" he asked. He looked at Martin, still curled in a ball, sobbing. *I'm going to have this bitch butchered when this is over.*

"Yes, my prey, and numbered," Raven replied. "Now what is the balance of the account you're drawing from?"

"Thirty-two million dollars."

"You will transfer all of it from that account to the one I gave you."

He looked at her with hatred in his eye. "You said one million fucking dollars—"

"I will feed you your dog's cock and make you swallow every morsel while he watches."

He dared to look her in the eyes, and his entire body shuddered with terror. *Her eyes are glowing yellow. What in God's name is she?* "God, this will ruin me." His trembling voice was barely a frightened whisper.

"Do not make me ask again, prey."

His fear at this point was palpable. After a few minutes of typing and code verification, the process was complete. He handed Raven her phone. "It's done. You have the money." He began sobbing, his face in his hands.

"You will, of course, understand if I don't take your word for it, prey." Raven accessed her account and saw the new deposit of thirty-two million dollars. She took an electronic device from her handbag and began typing at an incredible pace.

"You have what you asked for. Will you please let us live?"

She didn't respond for a few seconds, then she looked up. "I'm sorry, my prey. What did you say?"

He spoke with tears still falling from his eyes. "Will you let us live?"

"The game isn't quite over yet, my prey. I told you when this started that we'd have to play it out to the end. While my goal was never in doubt, the game has to reach its natural conclusion. Unfortunately for you, the next level is about to start. You see your dog on the ground all curled up and sobbing? It was used pretty badly by you. And what's fair is fair, so, to that end, I've always believed that turnabout is always fair play. So, now, to help alleviate the poor dog's misuse at your hands, he now gets to fuck you. Just as you politicians enjoy fucking over your constituents, he will literally get to return the favor."

Nathan stood and backed away, falling over the chair he backed into.

"No, no, no! Don't do this to me! Please God, don't do this! I gave you what you wanted!"

Raven held him down. "That is not how this works, my prey. You gave me nothing. I take what I want, and right now, I want to finish playing." She forced the senator onto his chest and held his head to the floor. "Come here boy" she called to Martin. "Come here boy, crawl to me boy."

On his knees, Martin crawled to where they were, his right arm dragged the ground, the broken bone looking like it might pop out of his arm any minute.

"Please God—"

"Silence, prey!"

"On your knees prey! Now, dog, you will feel no pain in that broken arm. Mount the prey and put your cock in his ass."

Martin forced himself to speak. "No . . . I don't want to do this—"

"Look at me, dog." Raven's eyes glowed like stars. "He made you suck his cock and he came on your face. Remember? Now it's your turn. Put that big dick up his white ass, and fuck him!"

Martin wiped his face and looked at his hand. It was covered with ejaculate. Intense anger and hatred overwhelmed him. He looked at Raven and stroked his penis until it was hard.

"Here it comes, my prey," she playfully whispered in his ear.

"Ahhh. . . Ahhh . . . Ahhh . . . Martin stop, plea . . . stop, Ahhh! . . . "

Still holding the senator's face to the floor, Raven looked up and watched as Martin forced his entire length into the senator. Her piercing eyes locked on his. "No, dog. Don't stop. Fuck him as long as you like. Punish him for what he did to you. Explode in his ass, dog. Make him bleed." Raven stood and walked to the bar. She took an unopened mini of champagne from the cooler, opened it, and drank from the bottle as she watched Martin pound into the senator.

"That's it, dog," she exclaimed, "go until you are exhausted. I do so enjoy the sound of his screams and the anguish of his cries. That's it, dog. Let it out, let it flow with all the force you can muster. Talk to me, dog. Let me know how it feels." She placed her hands on Martin's head and chin.

"Uhhh . . . shit! I'm cumming! . . . Uhhh!"

Snap! Martin's body went limp and fell forward, resting on top of the naked senator.

Raven placed a chair in front of the senator and sat down. "How was it, my prey?"

His only response was his infuriating crying.

Raven grabbed Martin's dead body by the shoulders and threw it against the bar. She picked the senator up and sat him in the seat across from her. Blood flowed down his legs and semen dripped from his penis.

"Now, my prey, who would you say has the control? And please stop your whining. It's annoying and it doesn't befit one of your station. Ha ha ha ha!"

Gasping, he said, "I'm . . . I'm . . . I'm going to kill you." His voice exhausted.

"Defiant to the end, my prey, but we both know that's an empty threat. I won't even take it to heart. Normally, if threatened, the one issuing said threat would find themselves dying in a very unpleasant manner. Come now, my prey, look at me. Let us have that pleasant conversation you spoke of earlier."

He looked at her. "What in God's name are you?"

"I am my mother's creation," she replied. "More than that you do not need to know. It is time for this to end, my prey.

"How does this end?" He quivered as he spoke.

"Well, let's see. I could simply walk away, leaving you here to explain how your dog's arm was broken and how it died, why it's face is covered in your cum, why its cock is covered in your blood and bile, and why you're bleeding from your rectum. Are you prepared to explain to your fellow senators and all who know you how these events came to be? How about that free-spirited wife of yours? Do you really want to try to explain these things? Or would you rather die and spare everyone the life-altering embarrassment and prison term for yourself that is sure to follow? Because I can assure you no one will ever know of my involvement."

"Just leave," he said, "You've taken everything from me." Tears fell down his face.

"Very well, my prey. I'll decide for you." She stood, grabbed him by the throat with both hands, and lifted him straight up off the floor. She held him at arm's length until his legs stopped kicking. She threw his lifeless body on top of Martin's.

"Now, I'll leave and return to the bar, my dear dead prey. Thank you for a most satisfying beginning to my evening." She washed her hands and left the suite.

"WELCOME BACK, RAVEN. Can I pour you another glass of champagne?" Diego asked.

"Yes, Diego. Thank you," she replied.

"How's your evening going so far, Raven? I hope you're enjoying yourself tonight."

"I am indeed. I see the bar crowd has thinned a bit."

Diego placed her glass on the bar and poured her drink. "The night is still young," he replied and walked away.

"Is anyone sitting here?"

Raven turned to the voice that asked the question. "No."

"May I sit here?" the young woman asked and noticed the one-hundred-dollar bills in front of Raven.

"You are free to sit where you like."

"Thanks. I need a drink. My boyfriend and I had an ugly argument on the phone, and I just had to get out of my room."

Raven said nothing.

DIEGO APPEARED. "Good evening," he said to the young woman. "I'm Diego, your bartender. Can I get you something to drink?"

"Yes," she replied. "I'll have a Margarita, and make it strong."

"Would you like to start a tab?" Diego asked.

"Yes, Diego. I'm Keiko, by the way, and here's my credit card for the tab."

He took her card. "Will you be dining with us this evening?"

"Yes, I'll order in a little while."

He placed a menu in front of her. "Very good." He left to make her drink.

Keiko turned toward Raven. "That's a gorgeous dress you're wearing. Is it a Versace?"

"It is." Raven responded without looking at her.

"Your Margarita, Keiko," Diego said. "Please let me know when you're ready to order. Enjoy your drink." He turned to Raven. "Raven, can I pour you another glass?"

"Yes, thank you, Diego." She pushed a bill toward him.

He took the note and walked away.

"What drink costs a hundred dollars?" Keiko asked Raven.

"The drink of my choice," Raven answered, annoyed. "And why is it any of your concern?"

"I'm sorry," Keiko said. "I didn't mean to offend. It's just that I was curious. I mean, you are a beautiful woman and you're here at the bar alone. I'd bet men worship the ground you walk on."

"I'm alone because I choose to be, and as for your last statement, I do not seek anyone's admiration."

Wow, maybe she's gay. As beautiful as she is, and the way I feel right now, I'd love to fuck her and I'm not gay.

Diego approached again. "Raven, the gentleman at the end of the bar would like to buy you a drink."

She looked over and saw a man hold up his glass, as if to toast her. "You can tell him 'no thank you,' Diego."

"Yes, ma'am."

"Wow, Raven," Keiko said, "Wasn't that a little bit cold? He just wanted to buy you a drink. He's hot. You not into Asian men? I would have accepted it."

Raven turned toward her and spoke in a soft voice, "You said your name is Keiko, correct?"

"Yes." She smiled at Raven.

"Keiko, we are not friends. Not only do I not need your advice, I have no desire to engage with you in any conversation. Not only am I annoyed at the sound of your voice, but your presence next to me has become irritating. I can't force you to move, but it would be in your best interests to take your drink and sit somewhere else." Raven looked away from the young lady and drank from her glass as the bartender approached.

"Diego," Keiko said, "I'll be moving to a table at the back of the bar. I'm ready to order some food." *Mean black bitch.*

"Very good," Diego said. "You can close out your tab and I'll have a server seat you."

"Thanks," she replied.

"Diego," Raven said, "I need some peace and quiet away from the irritants of this bar." She looked pointedly at Keiko. "I'll be going to my room to dine after one more glass. I'll call my order in from room 2106."

"Yes ma'am," he replied.

"Thanks, Diego," Keiko said. "I'm going to my table." *Mean bitch.* Keiko signed her receipt, took her glass, and walked away, obviously upset.

Raven finished her champagne and left the bar. Everyone in her vicinity took note as she walked out.

7

A KNOCK AT THE DOOR. Annoyed, Raven turned off the water running in the bathtub. She walked through the luxurious suite to answer the door.

"Who is it?" she asked.

"Room service."

She opened the door, and two men burst through, knocking her to the floor. Each man grabbed her by an arm, forced her to the living room area, and threw her on a sofa. They were quickly followed by two more people. The last intruder through the door closed and locked it.

"What is the meaning of this?" she asked in a defiant voice.

"You'll find out soon enough, but you might not like the answer," said a voice from behind her.

She turned to face it.

"You remember me?" asked the Asian man from the bar. "I tried to buy you a drink at the bar, but you refused my gracious offer. That really pissed me off. By the way, baby, my name is Hiroshi, and you are in a world of trouble."

A woman walked up and stood beside Hiroshi.

"Remember me, Raven?" Keiko asked, still clearly angry. "I was only trying to be nice to your black ass, and you threatened me. It doesn't matter now, anyway, because now you belong to us to do with as we please."

"What do you mean 'I belong to you'? Get out of my room now!" Raven glared at the men standing in front of her.

They didn't move and they said nothing.

"Or what?" Hiroshi asked. "I doubt you can force us out and you're here all alone. You should have kept your mouth shut at the bar about where to send room service. We took care of that, so no one will be knocking on your door." He pointed at his men. "You two. Help Keiko check out the suite."

Hiroshi turned his attention back to Raven. "This is a nice place you have here. My girl tells me you're rich, and from the looks of this suite, she might be right. She is right about one thing though. You are a beauty." His eyes took her in and undressed her simultaneously as she sat on the sofa with her arms folded across her chest.

"I told you, Hiroshi," Keiko said, returning to the living room, "this bitch has a closet full of designer clothes and shoes. Too bad none of it is my size." She carried three dresses she'd taken from a closet.

Raven turned toward her. "Put those back where you found them, you little thief!"

Hiroshi stood in front Raven. "Everything in this suite, including you, now belongs to us," he said. "Disrespect my girl again and that beautiful face of yours will be ruined." He smacked her across the face and sat down on the sofa across from her, an angry look on his face. Keiko sat on his lap. He took a large black gun from the small of his back and placed it on the table.

"Kento," he hollered, "what's the deal back there?"

"There is no one else here but us, boss," Kento called back. "It looks like she's here by herself. There was a stack of cash on the dresser in the bedroom. Jiro took it." Kento walked into the kitchen area and opened the refrigerator.

"Where the fuck is Jiro?"

"Taking a shit in the guest bedroom. This is a big fucking suite, boss. It has two big-ass adjoining rooms and a den."

"You must be rich," Hiroshi said to Raven. "Are you living here?" He picked up his gun and twirled it in a circular fashion.

She stared at the weapon and said nothing.

"Hey," he said. "I asked you a fucking question!"

She looked at him and still said nothing.

"Don't even think about reaching for my gun," he said. "You wouldn't even get close." He called for Keiko. "Keiko, baby, fix me a drink."

She stood and went to the bar.

Jiro came into the room. "Here, boss. I counted five grand. There may be more here." Jiro handed Hiroshi the money and went to the bar.

"So, Raven," Hiroshi asked, "is there any more money lying around, or jewelry, I need to know about?"

"Here, baby." Keiko handed him his drink and stood behind him, her hands on his hips.

"What do you think, Hiroshi?" Raven said calmly, in answer to his question.

"What the fuck do you mean 'What do I think?' That was a simple fucking question. I suggest you answer it." He grabbed his gun off the table and pointed it at her.

"Hiro," Keiko said, "let's just do this bitch and be done with her black ass. I'm getting bored."

"No, babe," he replied, "I have a better idea. "After we're done with her, we can make a lot of money off her. There's a huge market for young black American women on the Middle East circuit. We could get two hundred grand easy for her."

"Yeah, boss," Kento agreed, "You're right. We wouldn't even have to arrange for transportation. The rag heads would take someone like her in a heartbeat. We just warehouse her ass with the others for a few days. That is, after we have our own fun with her first."

"You three knock yourselves out," Jiro said. "I'm not into niggers."

Hiroshi turned to Raven. "Let me explain what's going to happen. You see, baby, we're Yakuza. You may have heard of us. We run all the crime in this—"

Raven laughed. "No, I don't believe I have. Is that a second-rate Chinese boy band?"

"You fucking bitch!" Keiko rushed toward her, wielding a knife.

"Oh, please." Raven rolled her eyes. With blinding speed, she stood, grabbed Keiko's knife hand, spun her around, and lifted her off the ground by the back of her neck. Both Keiko's hands instantly went to her throat.

"Put your hands down," Raven commanded, "or I'll break your neck."

Keiko's arms dropped to her sides.

"What the fuck!" All three men cried in unison, quickly pointing their weapons toward Raven.

She backed away, holding Keiko up higher with one arm but keeping them all in sight.

"Now," she said, "before your little manko (*cunt; translated from Japanese*) here suffocates, or one of you shoots her, or I break her neck, I suggest you each drop the magazines from your pop guns and eject the round in the chamber."

"The fuck did you just call her!" Hiroshi exclaimed. "You speak Japanese, bitch?"

"Damare!" (*shut your fucking face; translated from Japanese*) Raven responded.

"What the fuck! Who is this bitch!" Kento said. *This bitch gives me a fucked-up feeling.*

"Does it matter, Kento?" Raven asked. "None of you are in any position to do anything about it now. Now do as you're told, or she suffers horribly."

"Throw the fucking guns away now!" Hiroshi ordered.

Each of them dropped his weapon to the floor.

"Stop shaking her like that," Hiroshi shouted in anguish. "You're gonna hurt her!"

Raven slowly shook Keiko by her neck, left to right, like a ragdoll.

Keiko began to make gasping sounds, and saliva ran from her mouth.

"How the fuck can she do that shit!" Kento asked.

"Silence!" Raven ordered. "Now each of you remove your clothes. All of them! Now!"

"Fuck you, bitch!" Jiro responded.

"Take off your clothes or she dies," Raven replied.

"Take off your fucking clothes!" Hiroshi ordered his men.

"Good job, boys. Jiro, you made a comment earlier about not being into niggers. I take it you don't find the sisters sexually stimulating. I can tell you that, looking at what you have to offer, why, I don't even see a penis. A newborn baby has more dick than you. You couldn't come close to getting a sister wet, or any other woman for that matter, I'd suspect. Wouldn't you agree, Hiroshi? Kento?"

Each man looked, and even in their fright, each stifled the urge to laugh. Jiro used his hands to cover himself.

"It's all right if you two want to laugh, boys. All men are not created equal." Raven laughed.

"Please put her down," Hiroshi begged.

"Why should I do that? I'm enjoying this. I have each of you right where I want you. And she's not dead yet." Raven lowered Keiko to the floor and took hold of her hair. She began twisting it in her hand and closing her fist.

"Argh . . . Hi . . . Argh . . . Hiro . . ." Keiko croaked.

Raven pulled her head back and looked down on her. "Keiko, if I were you, speaking is the last thing I'd do. You should savor every breath I allow you to take. On your knees, Keiko." Raven now looked at the men. "Now, boys, I want each of you to sit down on the floor."

"I'm not doing shit," Kento said defiantly. "Why don't you come over here and make me sit down, so I can shove my dick up your ass?"

"Hiroshi," Raven said, "order him to be a good boy and sit down."

Hiroshi looked up at Raven. "Kento, she has Keiko, now sit the fuck down!"

Kento took a knee. His eyes were piercing, and rage filled, and they focused on Raven.

"Hiroshi, why do they obey you so obediently?" Raven asked.

"Because I'm their Oyabun, their leader. I run all Yakuza from South Carolina to Florida. Every member of our clan is sworn to obey me. Which is why you better kill me, bitch, because if I get out of this, you will be slowly slaughtered." He looked at her with hatred in his eyes

"That was a very stupid thing to say, Hiroshi," Raven said. "I'm sure it was to show your followers how defiant you can still be in the face of death. You four should have remained where you were, as your lives would have been considerably longer. I'm sure you all are aware by now that I am much than meets the eye. I enjoy hunting at bars, as it offers the anonymity required to do what I do. I heard you idiots as soon as you got off the elevator. Why is Keiko so important to you?"

Jiro and Kento looked toward Hiroshi.

"She is … special to me," Hiroshi nervously replied, "and that's all you need to know."

"Now, as for you, Keiko," Raven said, turning her attention back to the girl. "What made you choose me as a mark, from all the people at that bar? You may speak freely, but keep in mind that if you lie to me, I'll know."

"I thought you'd make a good slave girl for our house. If you had been nice to me, I was gonna change my mind and I probably would have chosen someone else. After we spoke briefly at the bar, and you pissed me off, I wanted to make you sorry for being such a bitch. And, since you were flashing your money around, I wanted it. I wanted to make your black ass pay." Tears fell down her face as she spoke.

Raven looked at Hiroshi. "A slave girl? You wanted to make me a slave girl? Very well. A large bill is about to come due." She smiled.

"What the fuck!" Hiroshi shouted and pointed his finger at Raven. He felt his heart pound in his chest. The others couldn't see what he'd just seen when he'd looked at Raven.

"What's wrong with the fucking lights," Jiro asked.

"I don't know," Kento replied. "Something is fucked up." He began looking around the room. All the lights in the suite began to flicker and then they went out. A sickening cracking sound was heard. The lights came back on.

"Ahhh! What the fuck did you do! What the fuck!" Hiroshi shouted too afraid to move.

"You may take your little manko back now. That is, if you still want her." Raven laughed.

Keiko's body stood upright, her back was toward Hiroshi, and so was the front of her face. Her right eye blinked once. Blood flowed from her mouth and nose. Her body slowly fell toward Hiroshi.

Projectile vomit erupted from Hiroshi's mouth. So fixated was he on Keiko, that Hiroshi didn't realize Raven was holding Jiro to her side by his throat.

"Ahhh . . . !" Hiroshi cried. "What the fuck, you fucking killed her. You killed her!"

Keiko lay with her face on the floor, the front of her body pointing toward the ceiling.

"You stay right where you are. Hiroshi," Raven ordered. "Get on your knees. I want you to fully appreciate Keiko's new configuration.

Why-the-fuck can't I move, Hiroshi thought in terror. *What the fuck is happening? Her fucking eyes, what the fuck is up with her fucking eyes? Akuma, fucking Akuma!*

"Oh, don't think I've forgotten you, Kento," Raven said. "As you can see, your penile-challenged friend here is having a little difficulty breathing at the moment. As you can also see, his face is getting puffy and he's as red as blood. You may have guessed that I'm slowly choking the life out of him. It's an excruciating way to die. I'm so enjoying it, though. Now, I think you said something about shoving your dick somewhere in my body? That was an awful threat to make. Don't you move either. I want you to see this." Raven walked toward him.

"Bitch I'm going to tear out your fucking heart and feed it to you!" Kento shouted with defiance, until he looked at Raven and terror overwhelmed him. *Akuma.*

"It's a good thing this room is soundproofed," Raven said. "Someone might have heard that and thought someone in this room was about to be killed. I think your little dick friend here his dead. Yes, he's about to lose his bowels. It's time to dispose of the body. Don't move now, Kento." Raven carried Jiro to the glass doors of the room's rear balcony.

"Hiroshi, Kento, say goodbye to your dead friend."

"You fucking bitch, you can't do this! Don't ! Hiroshi shouted.

"You're fucking dead, bitch!" Kento shouted. "You hear me? You're fucking dead!"

Glass from the doors exploded outward as Raven threw Jiro's dead body into the doors with such force it went five feet beyond the railing before gravity pulled it to the ground.

"Hiroshi! On your feet!" Raven ordered. "Crying over Keiko's disfigured body won't bring her back. However, if it'll make you feel better, I'll seat her next to you." She turned to Kento. "Kento, go to the kitchen and wait. As the head of the southern Yakuza, take your place of honor at the head of our dining room table. It's time to eat, and I'm starving."

Kento did as he was compelled to do.

Raven sat Keiko's dead body next to him and put a large plate on the table. Keiko's head fell onto the dinner plate, which soon filled with blood. Keiko's dead eyes stared toward the ceiling. The scene was grotesque.

Hiroshi sweated profusely, his fear palpable.

"Here's your water glass, dinner plate, and silverware." Raven placed the items in front of Hiroshi. She removed two chairs from the middle of the table and sat at the opposite end.

"You both are probably wondering why it seems you have no will of your own at the moment, other than to hurl curses my way," she said. "Well, let's just say, for the moment, that's the way I want it." She gestured to Kento. "Kento, look in that drawer below the microwave and take out the large carving knife."

He did as he was told.

"Now, Kento," Raven instructed, "take your place at the middle of the table. You can stand for this, since you'll be serving the first course this evening, and I don't want to hear you utter a single word."

He looked at her with all the hate he could muster. *Why-the-fuck can't I talk? How is this bitch doing this shit to us? I want to shove this knife into her fucking face.*

"Kento," Raven ordered, "put the knife on the table and take your dick in your hand. Get it hard for us, if you can. That's a good boy. Get it nice and hard. It'll make this so much easier."

Sweat poured from every pore of his body. *What the fuck is this bitch gonna make me do! God, what is happening!*

"Hiroshi, are you enjoying the show so far?" Raven asked. "I certainly am. Don't avert your eyes. I want you to watch Kento work."

Hiroshi looked at her, and the sight of her eyes terrified him.

"Kento, I don't think it's going to get any bigger, baby," Raven said. "It's leaking, and I don't want you to cum all over the table. Look at me, Kento. Listen to what I say, before you begin and follow my instructions exactly."

Her fucking eyes.

"I want you to take the knife," Raven said, "and put the blade at the base of your cock close to your body. Then, with all your might, pull your dick away from your body while at the same time pushing the blade across and down to cut your dick off. Do it quickly, and you shouldn't feel much pain. Please don't scream. I don't want the noise to spoil Hiroshi's appetite. After you cut it off, put it on Hiroshi's plate. You may begin."

Kento picked up the knife and placed the blade against his penis. His body was gleaming from the sweat that poured from every pore of his body. He trembled uncontrollably.

No . . . no . . . no don't do this shit, don't let this bitch make you do this shit. Ahhh . . . Ahhh . . . God . . . Help me . . . Ahh!

Hiroshi watched, frozen in absolute horror, as Kento cut off his own penis. Kento dropped the knife, placed the dismembered organ on Hiroshi's plate, and then slumped to the floor, his hands between his legs in agony, his mouth frozen in an unending, silent scream. He bled profusely from where his penis had been a few seconds ago. His blood quickly painted the floor crimson.

Vomit erupted from Hiroshi's mouth and onto the plate in front of him.

"Dinner is served, Hiroshi," Raven declared. "Now, pick up the meat on your plate and eat!"

"Fu—" Vomit poured from his mouth again. He looked into her eyes, picked up the dismembered penis covered in his own vomit, and placed it in his mouth.

"That's a good boy," Raven exclaimed. "I want you to try your hardest to suppress your gag-reflex until you've finished your meal. That's it. Chew and swallow. It looks like poor Kento may have had a heart attack. The blood has stooped gushing from the wound; it's only trickling out now. Tell me, Hiroshi, how does your friends cock taste?" She laughed.

He looked at her, his breathing heavy/ Sweat poured from his body as he chewed the flesh in his mouth. He violently threw his head back and grabbed at his throat.

"Argh . . . Argh . . . Argh . . . !" Projectile vomit again erupted from his mouth straight in the air. He fell backward in his seat and crashed onto the floor, his hands clutching his throat. His coughing became more violent.

Raven stood over him. "Hiroshi, you're choking on your friend's meat. How sad. I'm afraid I can't help, but for you, Mr. Yakuza boy band, this is a fitting way for parasites to die. If your men had checked all the closets in the master suites, maybe none of this would have happened. The true occupants of this suite are there, but missing their heads. Maybe I could have killed you all quickly and less painfully, but it wouldn't have been as much fun. Sometimes, that's the way these things go. You see, my original plan was much different. The people on this floor owe you their lives. So, your deaths have served a noble purpose. My original intention was to kill everyone on this floor, but since I got to play with you and your friends, my hunger has been satisfied—for now. Thank you for a lovely evening. Now, I'll go to my room and relax."

She left the suite, laughing as she closed the door behind her.

8

THAT UNGRATEFUL, two-timing bitch and her boyfriend had to die. I'm in bed convalescing, trying to get better so that our lives could go back to the way they were, and she's fucking him in my house. I'm home for weeks, bed-ridden, in horrible pain and alone. She wouldn't even sleep in the same bed with me. I'd just had major surgery, so when I was released from the hospital, I slept all day so my body could heal. I felt myself getting stronger by the day. She'd only come into our bedroom to change the sheets and would no longer help me to get out of bed to use the damn bathroom, but I knew something wasn't right. Even in my sleep, somehow, I could smell his stink all over her. To know what she was doing and I was helpless to stop it only made me angrier and filled me with rage, until the moment came when I caught her in the act.

"Oh . . . yeah, baby. Fuck me. You feel so good. Steve, I love your hard cock." Her eyes closed, and she moaned passionately. On her back, her lover's full weight pressed against her body. He did not respond verbally; instead, he stroked the pussy more forcefully and sucked her nipples vigorously. It drove her wild with desire to reach climax.

"Ahhh! What the fuck! Who are you!" she screamed, when she saw a man staring down at them on the floor.

"What's wrong baby—" He looked at her and instantly turned his head to follow her frightened gaze.

"Oh shit!" He jumped off her, and she instantly contracted her body to jump behind her lover.

"Don't stop on my account," the mysterious man said. "Please carry on. You had the balls to come into my house and fuck my wife in my living room so you may as well finish."

"I'm not your fucking wife!" she yelled. "What are you doing in my goddamn house!" *Jason's not built like him, no fucking way. That's not my Jason.*

"Look man—" Her naked, startled lover started to say.

"Shut the fuck up!" the man yelled. "Are you going to finish fucking her or not!"

"What do you want?" she demanded.

"Sarah, don't you recognize me? I'm Jason, the man you married, the man who loved you. Who was released from the hospital a few weeks ago, and who suffered from Parkinson's? Don't you recognize me? I think I'm cured."

"There is no fucking cure, and you're not Jason. Now get the fuck out of my house!"

"Look, man," her lover said, "whoever you are, you better get the fuck out of here before I kick your ass."

"Please give it your best shot, Steve—"

Bwok!

Jason didn't flinch. He looked at Steve's exposed penis. "Hahaha!" he laughed. "Is that the best you've got, you little baby dick motherfucker?"

Angered, Steve rushed in to strike again.

Jason easily evaded his clumsy attack. He then hit Steve so hard the guy was instantly rendered unconscious. Blood flowed from his nose and mouth and onto his crumpled body.

Jason now focused his anger on Sarah. "Now, as for you, you filthy, adulterous bitch, why shouldn't I break your fucking neck? How could you do this to me? Didn't I do all I could to give us a good life before I got sick? It wasn't my fault I was struck down with fucking Parkinson's. It's not that I didn't want you anymore. I couldn't perform with all the damn drugs I was on. So, the first chance you get, you fuck around on me? Or maybe you always have. And you do it in my house, with me upstairs, sometimes lying in my own shit because you were too fucked up to help me! It's been days since you last came into our room."

She backed away from him, using her arms to cover her breasts.

His anger intensified when he saw a white liquid flowing down her leg.

"Is he dead?" she screamed. "Who are you? You look nothing like my hus—" She screamed when he grabbed her by the arm and dragged her up the stairs.

"Do you see a body lying in the bed?" he asked. He threw her naked body on the bed. He opened a bottom dresser drawer, removed the bottom, and pulled out several envelopes. "These are our insurance policies. Who else knew they were there, except us? Here are life insurance policies, totaling five hundred thousand dollars. I guess you were waiting for me to die so you could cash them in."

She looked up at him in disbelief. "Jason, how—"

He looked at her and threw the envelopes on the floor. "It doesn't matter anymore, does it, bitch? Let's get you back to your fucking boyfriend."

He grabbed her by her long dark hair and dragged her out of the room, screaming." They reached the hallway banister. He lifted her body over his head as if she were a toy doll.

"No! No! Ahhh, Jason No don't do this to me!" Her screams stopped when her naked body hit the floor below.

I WAS SO ANGRY, Even after I killed them, that I took my sledgehammer and bashed in both their fucking heads until what was left was unrecognizable as human. I never saw so much blood in my life. It was everywhere. I never experienced that kind of uncontrollable hatred in my life. I went upstairs to get into the shower, and when I looked at myself in the mirror, I didn't recognize the face that looked back at me. Somehow, I'd changed. Not just my face, but my whole body. I knew the disease that had crippled me was gone. I felt more powerful than ever. After I got out of the shower, I knew I had to get out of there. I took all the cash I could find, packed a bag, and got the hell out of there. It was probably a dumb idea to leave that note, but I was furious. Now that I've had time to think about what I did, I'm frightened. I don't want to go to jail. I'm no killer, but now every cop in the state is looking for me. I've got to get out of the state, maybe head to Mexico once I get to Texas. The good thing is that I no longer look like the guy the cops are looking for, so my ID is useless. And besides, who looks for fugitives on trains? He put his now useless driver's license in his shirt pocket.

"Excuse me sir would you mind helping me with my suitcase?" the young woman asked him.

"Sure, not a problem." He stood and put her suitcase in the overhead bin.

"Thank you so much," she said, "and I apologize for disturbing you."

"No apologies are necessary. Are you at the window seat?"

"Yes. I'm Tiffany, by the way." She extended her hand.

"I'm Jason. Pleased to meet you, Tiffany." He shook her hand, and she took the window seat. He sat down and smiled at her.

"So, Jason, where are you headed?"

"To see my brother in San Antonio."

"That sounds nice. I'm getting off a little further south. I have a modeling gig that sounds promising."

They talked for a few hours more. The train continued its journey and wouldn't stop again until morning. As night fell, most of the passengers were asleep. Unable to sleep, Jason looked at his sleeping seatmate. His hands gripped his armrests, perspiration forming on his forehead.

"She reminds me of that fucking cunt I was married to. I thought she'd never shut up. I could break her fucking neck in a heartbeat. At least I wouldn't have to hear her goddamn voice anymore. In fact, I could kill everyone in this car, and no one could stop me. I've done it before, and it was easy. Now that I think of it, I enjoyed killing that bitch and her fucking boyfriend. Pounding their faces into hamburger was a rush. But . . . I can't do this. I have to fight this urge to kill. The cops are looking for me now. What is happening to me? What happened to me? I don't want to hurt anyone. But I'm not the same person I was. No one knows me now. How did this happen to me? I can't kill again; I don't want to hurt anyone. I've got to get off this train.

Jason's eyes opened, and he rushed from his seat. *That's it! That's the answer! Go in there and lock the door. Lock the door and don't come out. I've got to figure out what to do.*

The rest room door closed and the occupied light turned on.

9

DEEP IN A SOUTH American jungle, in the subterranean cavern, four hooded figures sat around the large stone table in the room lit by ancient torches. Each removed his hood, and one spoke for over an hour. The others listened intently.

"We must locate the patients that Laden implanted with my organs and transfused with my blood," Damon said, "and destroy them if they are still alive. Nothing like this has ever been done, and there is no knowing what these Homos may mutate into if they've survived. I have loaded all of Laden's notes and research into our analytic systems for analysis."

"Yes, and we will have an answer shortly, Damon," said Ogun. "You endured a harrowing experience. I am pleased you survived. Having heard your tale, it's no wonder we could not locate you, nor could I sense your presence."

"How did that fucking Homo die, my brother?" Shango asked, looking into his brother's eyes.

"Violently."

Shango smiled. "What about the one who hit you with his truck? He has to die as well!"

"I know of your contempt for the Homos, Shango," Ogun interjected, "but that can be dealt with at a later time."

"Have you fully recovered, Damon?" Nuru asked.

"Yes, both physically and mentally. Although it remains to be seen if there will be any long-term effects from having had many of my organs cut out and regenerated. Our physicians tell me my body is completely whole again and that I'm in perfect health. I feel fine."

"We must take steps to ensure that something like this can never happen again to any of our people, Nuru," Ogun said.

"It will be done, Ogun," Nuru replied.

"Now that the council is once again whole," Ogun said, "and we welcome the return of our brother, we must now bring him up to date on the events that have transpired. Which we know now may directly be linked to his disappearance."

"What has occurred in my absence, Ogun?" Damon asked.

"Around the time of your disappearance, when you didn't respond to my last call to form the council, I had begun to sense a presence in the world that was unknown to me," Ogun explained. "It was something evil and malevolent. It was weak at first, as if it were still growing. On the occasions when I would sense it, I could almost feel its power. After learning of what happened to you, I am now convinced that what I have been sensing is indeed the nascent presence of a Dark One, a Dark Mother."

"A Dark Mother!" Damon gasped. "Are you sure, Ogun?" Damon shuddered with trepidation. *Laden did transplant my heart into a female.*

"At this juncture, I am," Ogun said.

They all looked at each other.

"I know the ancient stories of the Dark Mothers," Damon said. "In fact, I recounted the tales to Laden before I killed him. But Ogun, how can such creatures exist today? No one, no record, was sure of their exact origins in ancient times. We do know that there are no more Dark Mothers. So how can we be sure that what you sense is one of these creatures?"

"I don't doubt Ogun's abilities," Shango said, "but those were my sentiments when Ogun proposed this theory in your absence, brother."

Nuru turned toward Shango but said nothing.

"No, Shango," Damon said, "it's not Ogun whom I doubt. But, to think that a Dark Mother could somehow exist today? How is that possible?"

Ogun explained. "Since our last meeting before you came back to us, Damon, I began extensive research using all the tools at my disposal to look into that very subject. My findings have led me to believe that those whom we called the Dark Ones, or Dark Mothers, in times past were far greater than any of the ancients knew. Their mental and physical abilities were far beyond any Protos of their times, but those that did exist were unstable. I have uncovered ancient records that point to our women's ability to use conversion as the reason the Dark Ones came into existence."

"Conversion?" Shango mused. "With our advanced science, conversion hasn't been practiced by our people in who knows how many millennia. Not only is it not spoken of today among our kind, it is a dead practice."

"Ogun," Nuru asked, "how is that possible? We even removed the Homos' limited ability to use conversion uncounted centuries ago. An ability they never knew they possessed themselves."

Ogun nodded. "That is true, Nuru, but do any of you truly know how conversion worked, even in its nascent beginnings? Or what it could bestow or the cost it demanded?"

No one spoke.

Ogun continued. "Just as we each serve a vital role on this council, as Nuru the Builder, Shango the Destroyer, Damon the Strategist, I am the Keeper of Knowledge that spans the vastness of all who have existed on this planet. As the Keeper, it is my task to be aware of all things and to maintain our vast reservoir of knowledge. What our ancestors called Conversion was a process by which a pregnant Proto, over time, could bestow upon her child in utero certain physical and mental characteristics and manipulate the fetus's physical form. Just as we can use science to correct any birth defects in both our young or the Homos. This ability served our population well for centuries, until we advanced to the point that none of our kind were ever born defective and our genetic structure was perfect. Some in our distant past, however, chose to take Conversion to its farthest limits. This occurred thousands of years ago, when we were at war among ourselves and destroyed all that lived. It was during this time that the Dark Ones began to appear. While we pitted the Homos against themselves and fought our own endless wars, some others took a darker path.

"I have uncovered ancient accounts of the birth of a Dark Mother. It is written that, at birth, the child would tear through the abdomen of its mother, who had been in a self-induced coma for the entire gestation of her term. During the last few months of pregnancy, the mother would speak aloud, as if she were having conversations with the unborn child. As if two distinct voices and personalities were engaged in debate. The thing that would be born appeared to be a newborn babe, but was far from it. It is written that anyone present, be they Homo or Proto, died without warning upon handling the child within days after its birth. As it grew, so too did its cruelty.

"It is written that these creatures were born with the ability to manipulate both the minds and bodies of others. Thus, making it child's play to hide in plain sight, allowing it to grow and become one with its surroundings until it struck. Just as it takes Keepers centuries to hone our mental abilities through intense study and meditation, these creatures were born with abilities far beyond the Mind Touch of a Keeper. They were said to have the ability to travel great distances in the cover of darkness and to hide within shadows. This account is known to all present. It was called the power of shadow. They were also said to have an ability to transfer their minds into the bodies of others. This was known as transference. An ancient Dark Mother was known to use this ability to transfer her essence into the body of a newborn child. Thus, the story of the firstborn Hebrew males being killed during the time of Pharaoh. Of course, that was for naught because all Dark Mothers were known to be female. The Dark One would reappear decades or a century later to resume her cruelty upon those that wronged or attempted to killed her."

"So, Ogun, these things were not invincible? Damon asked. "They could be killed?"

"Yes," Ogun responded. "It is written that, of the known Dark Mothers that existed, four were killed in battle, though it took centuries to accomplish. The method of death in all cases was beheading. But because they possessed the ability of transference, whether they stayed dead is a matter of conjecture.

"We do know for a fact that there haven't been any of these creatures around in millennia," said Shango. "So, what if one appeared today? We are not the Protos of ancient times. We have weapons that can vaporize anything on this planet, and we control this world. We need to find this thing and destroy it."

"To that end," Ogun said, "we will all remain here at my compound to plan and seek out this thing using all of our resources and once found destroy it. On that front, Shango, what is your recommendation?"

"Ogun has sensed this thing's presence in the US," Shango said, "so I think it prudent that we deploy K Squads armed with our most advanced weapons throughout the country so that they can be quickly dispatched when this thing rears its head. I also recommend that all our people worldwide be notified, so that when anything unusual occurs in their sectors, we will know instantly. We also need our people to take no direct action against it if found. We don't want this thing becoming aware of our people. Thus far, it's a safe bet that if it exists, it knows only of its fellow Homos."

Ogun nodded. "Wise recommendations, Shango. They will be implemented."

"Ogun," Damon said, "since these things are creatures of chaos and destruction, it would be wise for us to put our plans for the next great war on hold for the foreseeable future. If these creatures are as formidable as the ancient texts would have us believe, what better place to hide and spread their chaos than a world at war? Also, it would be best if we suspended the release of all Covid variants and put out the neutralizing agents."

"You are correct, Damon," Nuru said, "which is why the council has already taken the actions necessary to delay those plans. We have also halted all internet disruption campaigns."

"Now, my brothers," Ogun said, "we each have our respective tasks to perform. Each of you will tie in your command systems to my own so that we can monitor happenings from around the world from here and allow our AI systems to coordinate our efforts. We will not rest until the thing we seek has been found and annihilated."

Each elder rose from his seat and exited the massive chamber through four different doors.

LATER THAT SAME EVENING, Damon went to the living quarters of his brother.

"Damon!" Shango shouted, "Come in, my brother! Let us toast to your return!" He poured them both a drink.

They took their drinks and sat down.

"Damon," Shango said, "when this thing is over, we will slaughter the Homo that almost took you away from me—and his whole fucking family." Changing topics, he asked, "What is your take on this Dark Mother thing that Ogun is so worried about?"

"Ogun is not one to worry," Damon said, "nor is he given to flights of fancy. If he senses a threat to our kind, then it will be given immediate priority above all other concerns. Including a missing elder. Don't forget, brother, that Laden did implant my heart into a Homo female. If these things mutate the way our AI systems suggest, she could very well be what Ogun is sensing."

"Have you spoken to Nuru?" Shango asked.

"Yes, I have." Damon gave his brother a stern look. "And you cannot continue to challenge Ogun. He is the head of our council and has been for centuries. He is to be obeyed without question."

Shango held up a hand in protest. "All right, Damon, maybe I was out of line during our last meeting when he summoned us and told me he had lost contact with you. Then he tells us of this presence he senses, which now may be the emergence of something that even he can't identify. What was I supposed to do? Sit there and say nothing, when he tells me my brother may be dead!" His eyes flashed in anger.

Damon nodded slowly. "I understand your anger, brother, and your frustration, but Ogun is the Keeper, and you are well aware that he has knowledge of things we do not."

"And I am the Destroyer," Shango said, raising his voice. "It is *my* function to eliminate any and all threats to our people and our way of life. To eradicate anything that would impede the accomplishment of our goals. Those decisions are mine alone!"

"Yes," Damon said. "No one is questioning that we each have a designated function and responsibilities. Or that we can carry out those functions in our individual capacities without interference or in a coordinated effort to further our people's goals." He frowned. "However, once they are mandated by the council, there is no debate. The time for argument is over. Once we have decided on a course of action, it is done. The people accept our judgments and act accordingly.

"Remember, Shango. We four are the council, but Ogun is our leader. And that's as it should be. Shango, we do not challenge the Keeper. If he believes there is an imminent danger that must be addressed, then all other considerations are rescinded until the threat is neutralized. The Keeper has the right to override the council and act. It is our responsibility to carry out his orders in such an event. Ogun is the most powerful of us. You know as well as I do that he could neutralize any of us if he chose to do so."

Shango's eye flashed again in anger. "No Proto would intentionally harm another," he replied.

Damon sighed. "Under normal circumstances," he said, "you are correct, Shango. But over the centuries, you have expressed your dissatisfaction with Ogun on many occasions—to the point of outright insolence. This must stop, brother. Yes, you sit on the council, but you are the youngest of us, and while your voice is equal to ours, it does not supersede that of the Keeper. Once he chooses to act on his own authority, that is it. Rarely has that happened in our lifetimes, but it is his right. And you have no right to question him. If given sufficient cause, Ogun's Mind Touch could destroy you. His power is absolute, which is why Keepers have always headed the council. And it was Ogun who selected you to serve on the council all those centuries ago, as the Destroyer, and he doesn't make foolish decisions."

Shango shouted back, "Well, maybe the time has come to reexamine how the council functions. Regardless of all that you have said, my brother, I'm every bit as powerful as any of you. And I'm not intimidated by Ogun!"

"You may not be, brother," Damon warned, "but if you anger him beyond a certain point, you will come to regret it. I'm trying to see to it that you never experience the destructive power he wields. You have no clue what he is capable of, little brother, I do. So, as of this moment, you will cease your disrespect of his authority! Unless you are given cause that is plain for all to see, you will cease your contempt for Ogun himself, or it will be me who will have you removed from the council. Do not forget the power wielded by the Strategist! We can ill afford to have disruptive voices on the council when we need to be unified in times of imminent threats to our existence."

"Damon!" Shango gasped. "You would do that to me, your own brother? What imminent threat? This supposed thing that Ogun senses but can't identify?

Maybe his time as Keeper has come to an end." His contempt was palpable, but when he looked into his brother's eyes, they were cold and deadly serious. "All right, Damon," Shango said, now contrite. "I understand, brother, but it was not my intention to be defiant of Ogun. My emotions got the better of me when I thought you might be dead. I will speak with Ogun. A great number of Homos were gonna pay for your death at their hands."

They both smiled.

"And at least one still will, little brother," Damon said. "Before I left Laden's lab, I searched for my belongings and couldn't locate them. The Homo that hit me with his truck must have robbed me before he drove off. My watch, communicator, and ring were missing. They have all been deactivated, and even if they weren't, he wouldn't have a clue how to use them. I will be able to track him once this thing we are dealing with is over. Now that's out of the way, have you had time to read my report on the other experiments that were conducted using my blood and organs? Laden transfused sick patients using my blood."

Shango nodded. "Yes, I've seen the report, and our people have gathered up all the bodies and taken them to our facilities for analysis. One of those transfused patients was taken alive, although it didn't live long. We should have the result of its analysis soon. All evidence of the experiments and the patient's existence have been removed from all records, and the patients' families have been destroyed. All police reports and evidence surrounding the deaths caused by the transfusion experiments have been eliminated. Laden's doctor buddies who helped him with his organ experiments have all been disposed of and all their records erased." Shango got up to pour himself another drink. He handed one to Damon as well.

"We still haven't been able to locate the Homos that my organs were transplanted into," Damon said. "We were able to locate the families of the patients and they were all dead, which saved us the trouble of killing them. We do know that the experiments are now killers, as all the family members were killed in a most brutal and imaginative fashion."

Damon took a sip of his drink, then continued. "These were not your run-of-the-mill Homo killings. Some were slaughtered in a way that would make their primitive ancestors proud. It looks like the organ recipients may have somehow been able to disguise themselves in some manner, because we have no clue as to where they may be. One of them was an autistic child. Now where the hell could a helpless child with autism disappear to? Our AI systems suggest that genetic mutation has occurred in the transplant patients. If that's true, then who knows how dangerous these things have become."

Damon drained his glass and looked into its empty depths, lost in thought.

10

"SHIT," TYLER WHINED. "I'm bored to death, babe. This isn't doing it for me anymore." He poured another drink and went out to stand on the balcony of the luxury suite, fifty stories up and overlooking Las Vegas at night. The night air caressed his naked body.

"What would you like to do then, babe?" Amber asked. "I'm game for whatever you want to do." She walked up to him, and he turned to face her.

She let her robe fall to the ground and placed her hands around his dick. "I think this big boy needs to be fed," she said. "I'll suck it, and then I'll watch you fuck her." Amber's head turned toward the living room. "She's on the sofa waiting for you. She and I are the last ones standing. You've gone through the best girls in Vegas. None of them but us can satisfy this huge cock of yours."

She sat in front of him and began stroking his dick to get him hard. "What's wrong, baby?" she asked. "You never take this long to stretch out. It's okay, though. You can get hard after I take it down my throat."

He looked down on her, a look of disgust on his face. "You're not listening to me, goddamnit. I'm not hard because I don't want to fuck. I'm bored with his shit." He walked away from her and into the suite.

"What's the matter baby?" The other nude woman stood and turned toward him. The look in his eyes excited her.

"I'm fucking bored out of my goddamned mind. That's what's wrong."

She said nothing.

Amber approached, holding a drink in her hand, her walk unsteady. "Hey, baby," she said, slurring a bit. "How about this for excitement? We've watched you fuck girls bloody, and that was definitely a turn-on for me. That big-ass cock has made us both scream, but how about we change things up a little?"

Amber put her drink on the table and pushed herself in front of the other woman as if the woman wasn't even there. Staring at Tyler, she said, "How about you let us watch you put all that cock up a guy's ass? I'd love to watch the look on some faggot's face as you fuck him." She brought both palms up to her face. "Oh my god! In fact, I know a queen I'd like to watch get fucked," she squealed. "I can get him here in no time! Wouldn't *that* be fun, baby? You're a big macho guy. Wouldn't it be fun to fuck the shit out of a faggot?" She laughed and squealed again.

Tyler looked down at her and up again at the other woman. Rage began to build inside him.

"Did I hear correctly what the fuck you just said to me?" he screamed at Amber. "You'd love to watch *me* fuck a man! What the fuck makes you think that's something I'd want or would enjoy! You think I'm fucking queer?"

He grabbed Amber by her throat, instantly cutting off her air. He looked over at the other woman. Amazingly, she didn't flinch. The look in her eyes excited Tyler.

Tyler lifted Amber off the floor with one arm. Her legs began to kick in the air. The look of fury in his eye told Amber she'd made a horrible mistake.

The other woman walked up behind Tyler. Her left hand grabbed his hard dick, and she placed her right hand on his chest, her bare breasts against his back.

"No, baby," she crooned. "That's too quick. We have to make this pink bitch suffer first. And I know just where to start."

Tyler threw Amber to the floor and watched as the other woman took hold of both of Amber's arms and dragged her to the master bedroom.

Amber, now frightened out of her mind, cried out, her breathing labored and tears cascading down her face. "Wait, what are you doing? I'm . . . I'm sorry, babe! I didn't mean—"

"Bitch, shut the fuck up!" shouted the woman dragging her. She got Amber on the bed face down and held her down by placing her knees and weight on Amber's shoulders.

"So, what'd you have in mind, baby?" Tyler asked. He stood at the foot of the bed, his dick at attention.

"This bitch wanted all that dick up some faggot's ass, so since you've never gone there with either of us, why don't we let her experience it for herself. I'll keep this wrapped around her fucking neck while you fuck her." She threw the pillows to the floor, sat up against the headboard, wound a stocking around her hands, and pulled Amber to her chest, wrapping the nylon around her neck.

"This I'm going to enjoy, baby," Tyler said. The look in his eyes was manic. He began working is dick into Amber's ass. She instantly realized what was happening.

"Ahhh! Don't do this . . . it's too big . . . Ahhh! Ahhh! . . . Stoooppp! Ahhh!" Amber cried out in pain.

The other woman pulled Amber's head up, using the nylon around her neck. "No, bitch," she said. "Don't cry now. Isn't this what you wanted? To watch all that dick go up somebody's ass. Well, now you get to feel what it's like."

The woman turned to Tyler. "Put it all in, Tyler. Make this bitch suffer for even suggesting that dumb shit." She loosened the strap so she could hear Amber scream.

Ahhh . . . ! Ahhh . . . ! Ahhh . . . ! Please . . . Stop, God . . . Please . . . !" Her cries got louder.

"It's ok, baby," the woman crooned. "Your ass isn't bleeding that much yet. You've had dick up your ass before. You can cry on Mama's titties." She laughed and placed Amber's head on one of her large breasts. Then she watched as Tyler went to work on Amber's ass.

Amber's tears and saliva covered her breast.

"Is it good, baby?" the woman asked Tyler. "You enjoying tearing that ass up?"

Tyler said nothing; he just continued stroking that ass. His thrusts became so forceful that Amber's head was driven hard into the other woman's chest. The whole bed shook. Blood began to pour out of Amber, and her cries got impossibly louder.

"No, bitch," the woman said. "You making too much damn noise now." She held Amber by her face and looked into her bloodshot eyes. Amber's tears and the agonized expression on her face excited her. "Here, baby," she crooned to

Amber. "You wanna suck Mama's titty? It'll make you feel better." She laughed. "If you bite me, though, bitch, I'll choke the life out of your ass."

Tyler watched as Amber tried to suckle without biting the woman. He pulled out most of his dick so he could enjoy what he was seeing. The woman reached down to finger herself.

"Hmmm, yeah, baby girl. Keep sucking. It feels so good. That's it, right there. Don't stop!" Her eyes snapped open and fixed on Tyler's. "You ready to cum, baby?" she asked. "I'm ready to cum!"

"Ahhh! Ahhh!" Amber screamed with all she had left, as Tyler forced his dick in her ass. He held Amber so tight she could feel his powerful hands crushing her hips. Her screams were cut short by the tightening of the nylon around her neck.

"Shit, baby," the woman said. "I'm cumming—again! Goddamn! Ahhh, I never came that hard in my life!" she said and moaned with perverted pleasure. She breathed so heavily she had to take a moment to calm herself.

Her eyes met Tyler's again for the briefest of instants, and she saw something there that made her afraid.

"Is she dead?" Tyler asked. She lifted Amber's head using the nylon strap, and released it. Amber's head plopped down onto her chest.

"Yeah, baby," the woman said, "I think you fucked her to death." She laughed.

"More like you choked her to death when you came," Tyler said.

"Wasn't it good though, baby? We just gave a whole new meaning to sexual stimulation. We both came, and we took this bitch out at the same time." Her laugh was evil.

Tyler shoved Amber's body to floor like it was garbage. It made a thumping sound when it hit the floor. He pulled the other woman to him, and they kissed passionately.

"What are we gonna do about the body, babe?" she asked.

"You're really fine with what just happened?" He sounded unconvinced.

"She's not the first bitch I've had to choke out, and she won't be the last. She had no idea who she was dealing with when she invited me up here. I was gonna do her ass anyway." She smiled and looked up at him, still holding their embrace.

"My kind of woman," Tyler said. "Young, beautiful, and deadly if she needs to be."

"That's me all the way, baby, and I'm all yours," the woman said. She glanced at the nude body on the floor. "Still, how are we gonna get rid of that?"

"Why do anything with it? This suite isn't mine."

"Amber said her and her girls use it to have their fun when they weren't fucking the richest men in Vegas," the woman said. "When she brought me here two days ago, she said all she wanted was to eat pussy. I didn't give a fuck, as long as I was on the receiving end. Then she brought you and her girls in, and you destroyed all that pussy. Other than that, I have no idea who she is or was or whatever the fuck." She laughed.

"That makes it even better. Let somebody else clean this shit up. Let's go wash off her blood and we'll go to my place. It makes this look like a dump." He laughed hard and looked at the woman holding hm.

"What's your name, beautiful?"

"Simone."

11

OGUN TOOK HIS SEAT at the stone table and called the council to order. "We have matters of grave importance to discuss," he said, "but first, I know you are all aware of the most recent reports of incidents occurring in the southern states. Of these, only two are of any concern to us. First, Senator Porter of Georgia is dead. Damon, how was this handled?"

"My people did an excellent job of downplaying his death by natural causes in the press," Damon replied. "All the public knows is that a highly regarded member of Congress passed away in his sleep at home. Autopsy reports are completed and will be released to the public after he's in the ground. As for his detail, he was killed in the line of duty on an undercover operation."

Shango now issued his report. "Ogun, no members of Congress are scheduled for execution at this time. In fact, Porter was meant to play a significant role in our now postponed war designs. The way in which they were killed is something we wouldn't waste our time doing. Whoever killed that idiot sexually tortured him and his detail. Our analysis indicates that this was the work of one person. There was a female in the room, as we found a woman's lip prints on only one glass that had been used by her. Analysis of the air in the room revealed a compound we couldn't identify, but we're still working to categorize the sample. But with that idiot's sexual proclivities, it wasn't surprising there would be women involved somehow. Only his detail was seen on video, walking down the corridor to the suite where the senator was dining for the evening. Whoever did this was stealthy, because they got in and out without being seen. They were also physically powerful. Porter's detail should have been able to handle any average Homo, and especially a woman. The way they were killed suggests it was violent—and personal."

"Could the assassin have been female, Shango?" Nuru asked.

"Without proof, it would be hard to believe that an ordinary Homo female could do to the bodies what was done to them," Shango said. "Our women could have easily killed them both, but not an ordinary Homo. Considering that unknown substance found in the air, we can't rule out the possibility."

"However," Ogun said, "this would be child's play for a Dark Mother. I know we haven't conclusively proven its existence at this time, but three of the characteristics we know they possessed were female, stealth, and strength. It may be too early to conclude that one of these things walks among us, but we cannot dismiss the possibility." Ogun continued. "This brings us to the next matter requiring our attention. The Yakuza leader of the southern district and his inner circle were all killed in the same hotel complex as the senator. Our people were dispatched as soon as we learned who had been killed there. Now, do we conclude that this was mere coincidence? Or is there much more here than it seems? Shango, what do we know at this time?"

"Hiroshi and his inner circle, including his half-sister, were all killed and tortured in the same hotel the senator was visiting," Shango reported. "As you all know, all major crime in the country has been temporarily halted by our chaos squads while we deal with this issue. Hiroshi was a major figure in the underground, and he could only have been taken out if we gave the order. His crew was viciously killed by what we have concluded was a single assailant. An air sample taken from the room showed that same unknown compound present in the senator's suite. As you are all aware, we have satellite surveillance covering the entire planet, and every major building of consequence can be tied into our systems. Our surveillance showed the crew at the hotel's lounge, drinking and eating. Hiroshi's sister was seated at the bar, and then a short while later, they are all seen leaving the bar and getting on an elevator. They exit on the twenty-first floor, they go to room twenty-one-zero-six, and are not seen coming out again. The body of one of the crew was found splattered on the street. He'd been thrown through the room's patio door. We saw no one exit that room."

"That air sample ties the murders together," Damon said. "Were they the original occupants of that room?"

"No," Shango said. "Some inconsequential couple was assigned to it, and they were also found dead as well. In all, eight people were slaughtered in that hotel." Replied Shango.

"How were the other two killed, Shango?" Ogun asked.

"They were both beheaded," Shango explained. "Their heads appeared to have been ripped from their bodies. No Homo on the planet could have killed in that manner. To reiterate, we also found traces of the same chemical compound in the air. All the bodies were examined at our facilities and disposed of. Our people handled all the investigations, analysis, and cleanup. There was no media coverage of the body found on the street or the deaths in the hotel." Shango looked over at Ogun.

"Judging from the look in your eyes, Destroyer," Ogun said, "it seems you have reached some conclusions. Can you elaborate?"

Shango nodded. "Based on the findings of our people, I'm now convinced that there is indeed something out there that demands our immediate attention, and it begins at that hotel. Someone viciously killed multiple people at that hotel. The killings were sloppy and amateurish, as if the killer could have cared less about getting caught or dealing with repercussions. We need to find out who or what is behind this. The entire hotel complex is now under surveillance, and we have our people in place. Every landline, cell phone, camera, and TV—all their so-called smart tech—is being monitored. I can't say with any certainty that a Dark One exists, but whatever this is, it's something we've never encountered before. In all probability, it's female. We need to find and eradicate whoever or whatever did this. It may very well be that we are seeing mutations from Laden's experiments on Damon. You recall that the families of the blood transfusion patients were all savagely killed and those transfused with his blood are dead, with one exception. Until we complete our analysis of the one body we have, we can't know for certain. Do you have anything to add, Damon?"

"So far," Damon said, "we haven't been able to locate any of the three surviving organ experiments. It's as if they've vanished. We do know that they are out there, based on the deaths of those that were close to them."

"With that," Ogun said, "let us now discuss another matter that also is of great concern to us. Last evening, during my meditations, I sensed something unlike the powerful and chaotic presence that first alerted me to the possible existence of a Dark One. This presence was weak and filled with rage and uncertainty, yet for one brief instant, it radiated enough mental energy that I was able to discern it not only from our people but from the Homos as well."

"Do we know where this thing is, Ogun?" Nuru asked.

"Yes," Ogun replied. "Let us go to the control center."

"THE THING WE SEEK is in Texas on a train heading south," Ogun said, as they settled in around a screen at the control center. "The engine number is one zero six two, and as we speak, it is on the screen and all pertinent information about those on board is being displayed."

Each elder looked at the screen.

"The quickest way to stop that mass of junk is to derail it," Shango said. "We'd have the cover of darkness, and since it's going to be in open country miles from anywhere, we can have our people on scene at the exact moment it derails. We can take every passenger, dead or alive, to our facilities and have the site cleaned up in a few hours. I can get my people on it in a matter of minutes."

"Derailing it may not be the best option, Shango," Damon said. "If this is one of Laden's experiments, we must take it alive so we can study it. Now, that may take longer, but we can have our people on the ground intercept everyone that gets off at every stop. We know only one-hundred-and-fifty-seven passengers are on the train, and we have their itineraries. Therefore, all we need do is intercept departing passengers."

"That will take time, Damon," Nuru protested. "We could also stop it with a directed EM pulse. That will shut down all power sources on the train and neutralize all their electronics. We can then employ neural pulse paralyzers to render every Homo on the train unconscious, making it child's play for our people to search every car. The question is: how do we find the Homo we're searching for?"

Ogun spoke. "After we neutralize the train and render them all unconscious, as you suggest, we can use handheld bio scanners on every passenger. We wouldn't need to worry about the young children and teenagers. We know that certain organs were removed from Damon during the experiments, so we focus our scans on the lungs, hearts, and kidneys of the targeted Homos. Our organs and physiology are distinctly different from theirs, so it should be easy to identify our target if it was implanted. Once it's in our custody, we re-energize the train, release the Homos, and they go on their way, oblivious to what occurred. We will then bring the target directly to this compound for study."

"Ogun," Shango said, "there is something else we must consider. We know that a chemical substance, unknown to us, was found in the air in Porter's suite, and we don't know it's origin. Until we can identify it, we must assume that it is somehow related to Laden's experiments, if we believe something non-Homo slaughtered everyone at that hotel. Let us assume also that somehow the Homos we seek have indeed mutated in some way. We have no idea what their mere presence could do to ordinary Homos. If they can release unknown bio compounds in the air, those substances could have a mutagenic effect on ordinary Homos."

"Interesting, Shango," Nuru mused. "Are you suggesting that we bring them all to our facilities for study?"

"We could transport them after they're rendered unconscious," Damon said. "Keeping them comatose wouldn't pose much of a problem."

"No, Nuru," Shango replied. "That's not what I'm suggesting. We don't need all of them for study. I'm suggesting that, after we acquire our target, we employ an overhead molecular scattering field to destroy every Homo on the train. We erase every record of their existence and scrap the commuter train."

Nuru agreed. "In light of the possibility that these things could possess mutagenic properties, that would be a prudent precaution."

Damon also concurred. "A persuasive argument, Shango."

"What say you all?" Ogun asked. He looked at each elder.

"Agreed," replied Nuru.

"Agreed," replied Shango.

"Agreed," replied Damon.

"Damon, Shango, coordinate with your people," Ogun ordered. "I want this completed before the sun rises on that train."

"It will be done," said Damon.

12

"**GOOD MORNING, MA'AM,**" the front desk clerk said with a smile as she looked up at the woman in front of her. "How may I be of assistance?"

"Yes," the woman said. "When I checked in last night, I made a reservation for a car to take me around the city."

"By the way, that is a stunning outfit you're wearing," the clerk added.

"Thank you," the woman said. "Black is my favorite color.

"May I have your name, please." *She has a beautiful voice.*

"Raven."

"I have it here. If you will go over to the concierge's desk, they can assist you with your car."

"The reservation does show I requested a driver?"

"Yes, ma'am, it does. The concierge's desk is located down the hall to your left."

"Thank you." Raven walked away with a grace all who were present noticed.

"Good morning," she said to the concierge. "My name is Raven. I scheduled a pick-up for this morning."

"Yes, ma'am," the concierge replied. "Give me a minute while I check my schedule." He turned away from her to look at his paperwork. "I have it here. A reservation for a limo and driver. I believe your car is waiting outside. Let me go check." He walked outside, looked to his right, and signaled for the car to pull up.

Returning to the desk, he said, "Ma'am, your car is pulling around. While you're out for the day, may I make dinner reservations for you this evening at our restaurant? The Four Seasons has the finest Steak House in the city."

She looked straight ahead as she answered. "That will be fine. 10:00 p.m."

The car pulled up and stopped at the entrance.

"May I tell the driver your destination?"

She handed him a fifty-dollar bill. "The St. Louis Zoo."

He opened the car door. After she got in, he told the driver her destination.

The limo pulled away. "We're about twenty miles from the zoo," the driver said, "and they don't open for another hour. Would you like to stop somewhere? I'll buy us breakfast."

"No," Raven said.

"All right," the driver said. "The zoo it is! But what's a fine sister like you want at the zoo anyway? Only white people go to the zoo. You should let me take you to some fun places. I'll show you a good time. In fact, why don't you sit up here with me?"

"If this is your attempt at small talk," Raven said, "you have failed miserably. The ignorance with which you speak befits a dolt like you. I am not a plaything, nor do I have any intention nor the inclination to lower myself to your level of stupidity. I hired this car to take me where I need to go, not to speak with its operator." Her tone turned icy. "Now, it would be in your best interest to do as I say and to keep your mouth shut. Trust me, you wouldn't like the alternative. Do I make myself clear?" She removed her sunglasses and looked into the rearview mirror.

When their eyes met, fear coursed through the driver's body.

A short while later, the limo pulled up to the entrance of the zoo.

Twenty minutes later, Raven got out of the vehicle. "You will wait here until I return," she ordered.

"Yes ma'am," the driver replied.

Raven closed the limo door and walked up the long sidewalk to the zoo's entrance. She stopped to read the various exhibit plaques and location maps. She found what she wanted and proceeded to her destination.

THIS IS THE FOURTH TIME this year I just happened to be selected to come to this damn zoo and take photos of these fucking animals and the stupid idiots that flock here to see them in cages. I didn't spend years studying journalism to waste my life doing this crap. The city paper was the only place that would hire me though. 'You need more experience'; 'you need more of this or that' was the bullshit I kept hearing. That blue-eyed bitch Chloe started the same time I did, but she gets assignments that got her noticed. I'm sure by sucking somebody's dick. I thought this was supposed to be a white man's profession. All right, dude. The faster I get this shit done, the faster I'll be out of here. They know me personally at the public relations office.

"Good morning," he said to the receptionist. "I'm Dave Beam. I'm a photographer with the City Paper. I just need to pick up my press pass."

A few minutes later, a young woman came out of the press office. "Good morning, Dave," she said in greeting. "Another photo shoot today?" She handed him his press credentials.

"Yeah." He grimaced. "I'm becoming a permanent fixture here, Sara."

"It's not that bad," she said. "At least it's a nice clear day and you get to go places the visitors can't."

"But there's nothing new to see," he complained. "I've taken hundreds of photos of this place, and it's boring. Now, maybe if you let me take you to lunch today, after I'm done, that would certainly brighten up my day." He smiled.

"That depends on how much of my own work I can get done before noon," she replied. "I'll let you know."

"You always say that, Sara."

"This time I might mean it," she said. "You aren't the only one looking for a promotion." She laughed.

"You're breaking my heart, Sara," he replied, and walked away. *Bitch.*

"Okay," he said to no one. "First up: the Giant Pandas. Again." He headed for the Panda exhibit. "Hmmm . . . lots of people here today."

"EXCUSE ME," THE WOMAN asked the groundskeeper. "Can you tell me which way to the big cat exhibit?"

"Yes," he replied, "Stay on this path and you'll run into all the big cats—the leopards are at the end." *Goddamn that sister is fine,* he thought.

"Thank you." She proceeded forward, stopping when she got to the lion enclosure. She removed her shades and stood facing them. A large male lion some distance away turned toward her.

"You are a magnificent creature," she said in a low voice.

The large cat slowly walked toward her.

"Do not come any closer," she said. "Let me admire you from here."

The large male stopped walking and was soon joined by two females. All three fixed their gaze on her.

"You are death times three," she exclaimed. "A wonderous sight to behold! I wish there were a way I could release you all from your captors so that you could punish them all. I cannot do that, because it would mean your deaths." For twenty minutes, she held the lion's gaze, seemingly oblivious to the many people around her who took note of her as she studied the lions and they her.

"They must like you, lady," a young voice said. "Those three are staring right at you."

She looked down. "No, little one. It is not joy with which they stare but longing. Longing to be free, as they should be, in their native land." She returned her gaze to the cats.

"Come on, baby. There is more to see." The mother of the child pulled him away.

His soft voice faded as they walked away. "But Mama, you said you liked the lions . . ."

Her gaze locked on the large male. "I must go now, great one," she said to him. "Find what peace here you can. I am truly sorry I cannot help you." She replaced her shades and walked away.

"Well, that was *different, and a bit strange. A beautiful woman like her, staring at the cats while they stared back at her. That is some different shit. She didn't say a word except to speak to that little boy. It made for a few good shots, even though I have no idea what she said to him. The kid's mother yanked him away in a hurry. Hell, I'm sick of this already.*

"All right, let's see how these last few shots came out. The lighting is excellent and—what the—!" He quickly looked up from his camera and frantically turned his head from left to right.

AFTER A COUPLE OF HOURS, Raven stopped at her last destination and sat on a bench facing the last big cat exhibit. She removed her shades. The people who passed her quietly marveled at her beauty. She seemed to not notice any of them. She walked over to the Leopard exhibit and found a space to stand. Her eyes soon found those of the big cat.

In a barely audible voice, she called to the cat. "Yes, come to me." Her voice was barely a whisper.

The large black cat approached as if he were stalking prey.

"You are indeed a beauty."

The large male bared his fangs, as if to give a warning.

"Magnificent, my beauty. You are without fear, and yet you elicit terror in others. Come, let me bask in your glory."

The cat stopped a few feet away from the glass enclosure, his piercing eyes on hers.

"Where is Titan?" Carol asked. "It's his feeding time."

"I don't see him," Michael replied. "Oh, wait. He's on the hill at the top of his enclosure."

"I see him now," Carol said. "Is that a woman standing there?"

"It looks like our boy found himself an admirer," Michael said. "One he likes, because he's not hissing."

"You would be mine, my beauty," Raven said to the big cat. "Of all your brethren I've visited today, only you move me. You are death that stalks the night, as am I. Let me savor those beautiful green eyes for a moment longer." After several minutes, Raven replaced her shades and walked away.

"Hey, Sara," Dave said. "I want you to take a look at something." He held up his camera so she could see the screen, excitement in his voice.

"Sure," she said, "What you got? These better not be pornographic pics." She laughed.

"I wouldn't do that," he chided. "Just tell me what you see in this shot." He smiled.

"It looks like a mother and her son, holding hands, at the lion enclosure."

"You don't see anything else?"

She got closer to him. "No. Am I supposed to? Let me see: I see the lions sitting on their butts looking ahead. Other people in the background, trees, and the sidewalk. That's about it. What am I supposed to see? It's a good shot from that angle though. Are you calling it quits for the day? If you still want to do lunch, I'm free."

"Oh, no Sara," he said. "I can't. I have to get back to the paper. I got called for another assignment. I'm gonna hold you to that lunch date though. I gotta run." He handed her his press pass and left.

DAVE MADE HIS WAY quickly to the park's entrance and found a seat just before he got to its exit. *I hope like hell she's still in the park! This is huge. Sara didn't see what I know I saw!*

He looked through all the shots he took at the lion enclosure and stopped on one. He sat back on the bench and continued to scan his surroundings. Soon, the object of his search came into view.

"Here she comes," he said out loud. "She's still here! Excellent! She's a lot taller than I thought." *She is a beautiful woman. I know what I'll do, just as she passes me.*

"Good, afternoon ma'am," he said. "May I ask you a question?"

Raven stopped and turned toward him. "Yes?" she replied.

"May I take your picture? I'm a reporter with the City Paper, and we're doing a story on the zoo's newest exhibits. I'd like to get some shots of the zoo's guests."

"No," Raven said. "I don't have time for that . My car is waiting." She turned to leave.

"It would only take a few seconds," he pleaded.

"Young man," she said. "I'm trying to be polite. I suggest you accept my answer, unless you wish me to be impolite." She walked away.

"Sorry, ma'am. You have a good day." His camera silently took photos as she walked away. He surreptitiously followed her and watched as she got into a black limo.

I don't know who you are, beautiful, but now I have a place to start. You'll be seeing me again real soon. This is gonna make my career.

13

*I*T TOOK A BIT OF TIME *and a lot of money to track down that limo driver, but working with investigative reporters sometimes pays off. It'll all be worth it if I can find her. I had to pay that driver three hundred bucks before he'd tell me where he picked her up. He also said she wasn't the nicest person he'd ever met and that she gave him the creeps. She turned me down flat at the zoo. We'll see. The Ritz-Carlton Hotel? At least she has good taste. This place is huge, but I'll walk around all day if I have to and talk to every employee I can find. A woman who looks like her is hard to miss. If she's here, I'll find her.*

"Good evening," the bartender said. "I'm Rick. Can I get you a drink?"

"Sure, Rick. I'm Karson. I'll have a Stella on tap."

"That'll be twelve even. You want to start a tab or pay as you go?"

"I'll pay as I go, thanks." *At these prices, I won't be here long. Let me see if he can help me.*

"Your change, Karson. Would you like to order something to eat?"

"Not right now," he said, "but I'd like to ask you a question."

"Sure, what you got?"

"I'm a fashion photographer, and I happen to know that one of the hottest models in the country is staying at this hotel. I'm hoping I might get to meet her so I can show her my portfolio, maybe land a photo shoot. I was hoping maybe she came in here."

"I see a lot of pretty women come in here, Karson. What does she look like?"

"Dude, if you saw her you wouldn't forget her. She's black and has the most beautiful brown skin you've ever seen. She's about six feet tall, jet-black straight hair that falls below her shoulders, piercing light brown eyes, perfectly cropped eyebrows, and her jawline is feminine, but slightly square and she is always immaculately dressed."

"Wow, that's a hell of a description. I'd love to see a woman who looks like that. I don't recall anyone coming in here that looks like that. There are six bars and restaurants in this complex. The Sea Cliff, where you are now, doesn't get many players in here. We're more a laid back, everyday-kinda-guy type of bar. You may want to try Neptune's Cove, on the fortieth floor. If she's a player, that's where she'll eventually show. Hey, by the way, what's her name so I can google her."

Shit, I don't know any model's names. Think, goddamnit. "Her name is Imani."

"Okay. I'll have to check it out."

"Thanks, Rick. I'll give the Cove a try." He drank from his glass.

"No problem, bud, but you may want to change into something a little more appropriate. The Cove's guests are a bit uppity, if you know what I mean." He left to wait on other customers.

"Thanks."

I have a jacket and slacks in my car. That will have to do. If I have to sit there all night I will, even if my credit card has to take a hit.

"That is a fabulous evening gown you're wearing," she said, complimenting the woman she sat next to. "Black looks good on you. Is it an Armani?"

"Thank you, it is," she replied and looked at the bartender, who was some distance away. He pointed to her and mouthed the words, "I told you." And laughed.

"I'm sorry. Where are my manners? My name is Helen." She pulled back in her seat, moved her long blond hair away from her face, and looked directly at the woman she spoke to and extended her hand.

"Good evening. My name is Raven." She shook the offered hand and turned back toward the bartender, who was still smiling as he walked up to her.

"Raven. How mysterious," Helen replied and smiled.

"私はあなたのために干渉を実行する必要がありますか？ ("Should I run interference for you? asked the bartender.) Translated from Japanese

"いいえ、大丈夫だと思います。彼女が耐えられなくなったら、お知らせします」 ("No, I will be fine. I'll let you know if she becomes intolerable," Raven replied.)

「シャンパンをもっと注いでもいいですか？ (Can I pour you more champagne?)

「はい」 ("Yes.")

He filled her glass and turned to the other woman.

There is something not quite right about you, Kenji. Your scent is somehow different from everyone else here. I have not encountered this before. It seems there may be more to you than meets the eye.

"Good evening, ma'am. My name is Kenji. May I get you a drink?"

"Yes, Kenji. I'll have a Margarita."

"I'll be right back with your drink."

"Impressive, Raven. You speak Japanese. Was any of that about me? Kenji is tall and kinda cute though, for a Japanese guy. If that's your taste."

"What makes you think I was talking about you?"

"I don't know. Just curious."

"As a matter of fact, some of what I said was about you," Raven stated bluntly.

"Would you care to share it with me? After all, in a social setting, it's not very polite if we're all not on the same page."

"You were not invited into the exchange. So what you think is of no concern to me."

"Don't be like that. I won't be offended. What did you say?"

"You will find out if it becomes necessary. And as for your comment concerning Kenji, he is a handsome man period, and a warrior's blood courses through his veins. You obviously wouldn't know anything about that. I can respect a man like Kenji. It is also clear exactly where your tastes lie." Raven drank from her glass.

"How would you know anything about where my taste in men or anything else lies? Hey, if you like him, that's fine with me." Kenji placed her drink in front of her and left.

"I said I respected Kenji. Nothing more."

"I like you Raven," Helen said. "It's refreshing to hear a woman state what's on her mind, social niceties be damned. So, are you here on business or pleasure this evening?" She drank from her glass.

"Neither."

"Raven, are you a model or an actress by any chance? I mean, your posture is perfect, your hair and skin are flawless, and you have excellent taste in clothes. There are a lot of movies and television shows filmed here in Atlanta. In fact, there is an industry production conference at this hotel this week, and there are quite a few industry players here this evening." *If she isn't, the bitch has the arrogance of a fucking super model.*

"To satisfy your curiosity: no, I'm not a model or actress. I wouldn't know anything about what is and isn't filmed here, and I find personal compliments vexing."

Helen was caught off guard. "I apologize if I made you uncomfortable. It's just that a woman as—Well, you know where I'm going. I'm here on business. I happen to be a television producer. That's why I asked if you were in the business. You certainly should be."

Raven drank from her glass and turned toward Helen. "And why is that? What makes you think that you would have anything I'd want?"

"You'd be a natural, either in print or on film. The second I saw you, I knew I had to meet you. I've guided the careers of many women in this industry, and none of them could touch you. Raven, you have what it takes to make it in my world."

Raven faced Helen. "There is nothing about your so-called world I would find appealing. I prefer the world I have created for myself. It does not include me parading myself around like a lap dog to satisfy the proclivities of others. I do not bow to anyone, nor will I make myself available to satisfy the petty impulses of others. My fate is my own, and I would not tie it to another under any circumstances. 今、あなたは私をかじり始めています。" (Now you are beginning to annoy me.) Raven finished her champagne and looked for the bartender.

"Do I want to know what you just said?" Helen's smile was uneasy.

"Would you like to?" She looked Helen in the eyes.

"I'm really not sure I want to know."

"I am sure. I said you are beginning to annoy me."

"I apologize for disturbing you. I'll leave you alone. Enjoy the rest of your evening." *Bitch.* Helen took her drink and left the bar.

"Raven, more champagne?" Kenji asked.

"Yes, thank you."

"Where's your friend?" He gave a mischievous smile.

Yes, there is something different about you Kenji.

"I was able to convince her to move along."

"Well, Raven, you must know that you could never sit alone for long without someone trying to engage with you in conversation. Every person at this bar, all fifty of the ones that can see you, have taken notice, and you are most noticeable. What you need is your own personal Samurai. I'll put a decoy drink at this seat so no one sits here." He poured her champagne.

"Are you volunteering, Kenji?"

"If it were possible, I'd take that job in a heartbeat." He left to wait on other patrons.

"GOOD EVENING, SIR, and welcome to Neptune's Cove. Do you have a reservation?" the hostess asked.

"No, I thought I'd just sit at the bar."

"I'm afraid the bar is full this evening, and it also requires a reservation after 8:00 p.m. If you like, I can put you on the waiting list. What is your name, sir?"

"Karson. I forgot to mention that I'm supposed to meet a friend here this evening."

"What is your friend's name, and I'll see if they are still here." She waited for his response.

"Would it be okay for me to just look inside? I might see them."

"All right, but if you don't find who you're looking for, you have to come back and wait to be seated." Her voice was stern.

"Understood." He walked inside.

This place is packed tonight. Now I see what Rick meant. This place is way out of my league and price range. I just hope she's—There she is! Now it's time to put my plan into action! This is going to be fun. Maybe I'll just slip this to the bartender and wait.

SEVERAL MINUTES LATER, Kenji returned. "Raven, this was left for you at the entrance. It seems you have an anonymous admirer now, one not brave enough to introduce himself face to face."

She turned it over in her hand. "A blank envelope. Kenji, I don't have time for this. Please take it back or throw it away."

"Come on, Raven, have some fun with it. Open it. See what's inside." He laughed softly.

「ケンジが好きなのはいいことだ」(It's a good thing I like you Kenji.)

「光栄です。(I am honored.) He replied with a slight bow.

She opened it. "It's a photo."

"What of?" Kenji asked, and filled her glass.

"An adult and child standing in a park."

Curious. I know exactly where this was taken. She handed the photo to Kenji. "Looks like some place at the zoo. I have no idea what this is supposed to mean."

He handed it back to her.

"Who gave you this?" She turned the picture over.

"The maître d'. Should I take it back to him?"

"No. I think I'll find out who this admirer is myself. Please hold my seat."

"Excuse me where can I find your maître d'? I have a question for him."

"Yes, ma'am, you'll find him near the entrance, standing behind his podium."

"Thank you."

He saw Raven as she approached him. "How may I help you?" *She is breathtaking.*

"Who gave you this envelope to deliver to me." She held it up. Her voice was calm.

"A young man, a few minutes ago. He said you were friends, that you'd understand."

"Where exactly is my friend now?"

"He said he'd wait for you in the outer lobby."

"Thank you."

Raven walked out of the restaurant and turned right. The people around her all turned their heads when she walked by them. As she passed the elevators, the outer lobby came into view. A man stood up and she approached him.

"Are you the one who sent this photo to me?" she asked.

"Yes, I am. My name is Karson. I'm very pleased to meet you." *She is gorgeous close up, and I don't think she recognizes me.* He held out his hand.

She looked at his hand without taking it and threw the envelope on the table. "What is it you want?" She folded her arms across her chest.

"We need to have a conversation. There is something important we should discuss."

"We do not need to discuss anything. You will tell me what it is you want and the meaning behind that photo."

"Could we go sit at a table? I want to show you something."

She followed him to a quiet corner table and they both sat. "My patience is growing thin. What is this about?" Her voice was intense.

"I'm a reporter for the City Paper—"

"The last time you spoke to me, you said you were a photographer assigned to take pictures at the zoo. Now which lie is it?"

He felt his heart beat a little faster. *Shit. She remembered.* He fumbled to take a folder out of his shoulder bag. "All right," he said, "Give me five seconds. I was at the zoo taking photos, and I took quite a few of you at the lion enclosure when you spoke to that little boy, and when you were staring at the lions. I took a lot of pictures of you. The thing I can't explain is why you don't show up in any of the pictures I took of you. The backgrounds are there, the foregrounds are there, people around you are there. The only thing that's not where it's supposed to be in these images is you. And I can't explain that, so I was hoping you could." He stared at her breasts as she sat down and looked at the photos on the table. A wicked smile swept onto his face.

"How did you find me?" She spoke without looking up.

"I may not be a reporter, but I work with the best, and I've picked up a lot along the way. It wasn't that hard, and a woman who looks like you is hard to miss."

"I will not sit here any longer and listen to this nonsense. Perhaps you should invest in better equipment? Do not attempt to contact me again." Raven stood to leave.

"Leaving now would be a bad move on your part."

"Please tell me why."

"I don't think you'd want me to go in there and show your friends these photos. Unless, of course, you can explain why you can't be photographed."

"Either you're the biggest idiot I've ever encountered, or you think I am."

He took a thirty-five millimeter camera out of his bag. "Maybe this will convince you." They watched a video.

"So, what do you have to say now? This was recorded just now, as you walked toward me. And, by the way, that is a beautiful dress you're wearing this evening. I'd love to get some shots of you with or without it on. Now that we're becoming friends, I just remembered something. You never told me your name."

She looked up from the camera. "My name is Raven." *This is very interesting; indeed, I was unaware of this aspect of who I've become. I will need to find a way of explaining this in the future, should the need arise. I know. It's the perfect ploy. Exquisite.*

"Now, Raven, is there any explanation you can give me for why you can't be photographed, or videotaped?"

"You work with these toys every day, and you have never encountered advanced jamming devices that render these things useless?"

"Of course, I've heard of sophisticated electronic systems that can do that, but we're talking military grade and top-secret government issue. As beautiful as you are, I don't think you have the means. No, there is more to you than meets the eye. So, would you like to explain?"

"You have no idea what you're talking about. Since you brought this to my attention, with ulterior motives of your own, I will share this with you. I am so much more than you could possibly imagine. Karson, do you have a cell phone?"

"Of course I do."

"You will see how wrong you were about these photos. Are you sure you don't see me in every shot? I'm going to stand by that wall, and I want you to take as many pictures as you like with your phone." Raven got in place and posed for him.

He began taking pictures. "Excellent, baby. The camera loves you. What? But how? You're in every shot."

Raven sat back down. "Tell me what you see on your phone Karson."

He had a confused, dumbfounded look on his face. He looked up from his phone to the photos on the table and back again. "I see you in all the pictures now, but how?—Wait, you're still not in any of the earlier pics." He picked up a photo off the table.

"Are you sure, Karson? Look at it closely and tell me what you see. Am I not in the photo?" Raven smiled.

"This is at the zoo. You're in front of the lion's enclosure. How?? You weren't there before. I know you weren't!'

"What am I wearing, Karson, standing in front of the lion enclosure? Tell me what you see."

"You're standing there in—what the fuck? The same dress you have on now. What the fuck! How? This is not right. You're in all the photos now." He stood trembling as he looked from one picture to the next. Perspiration formed on his forehead; his heart pounded in his chest. He looked at Raven, astounded.

"Sit down, Karson!" she commanded him.

"How? I've looked at these pictures all day. I know what I saw."

"Have you shown anyone else these pictures?"

"Yes. One other person and she didn't see you in the picture at the lion enclosure either."

"All right. That person is of no consequence. You, however, will have to be dealt with severely.

"What do you mean by that?"

"Look at your pictures again, Karson, and tell me what you see."

He quickly looked at all his pictures and immediately stood up. "You're not in any of them just like when I first took them. What the hell is going on here? What is this?"

"Sit down and don't move!" she said in a low voice. "Now, isn't that why you sought me out? To get those answers?"

"Yes."

"So, here is your chance to find the answers you seek. First, let me ask you a question. How old are you, Karson?"

"Twenty-four."

"In the prime of life. It's too bad your life is going to end so young."

"What do you mean my 'life is going to end so young.'?"

"It means exactly that. You are going to die tonight."

"You're fucking out of your mind. I'm out of here—" *Shit. I can't stand up. I can't move at all. What the hell is she doing to me?*

"Are you finding it difficult to move?" she asked. "Remember: I told you to sit and don't move. At this point, you can't do anything I don't allow you to do. And don't bother calling out for help. Now, you went to a great deal of trouble to find me, so let's begin. You can relax. No need to be so tense. And keep your volume conversational. Now, what would you like to know about me?"

He looked down at his photos and back to Raven. He could feel his heart beating a little faster. "How can you be in the pictures one second and gone the next? How is that possible?"

"It's not possible," she said. "What you initially saw was correct. Look at them again. As you can clearly see, I'm not in any of the pictures you took."

"How? Is this some kind of trick you're pulling on me?"

"It's no trick. I can make you do anything I want. I can make you see anything I want. Let's call it my special gift. It's one of many."

"What are you?" Fear rushed through his body.

"I'm as human as you are. Well, maybe a little more. What did you think when you first saw those pictures?"

"I don't know. Maybe you were—I don't know what I thought, because it didn't make any sense. When I saw you at the zoo exit, I took more pictures, and you didn't show in those either. I thought I was losing it. When the limo driver opened the car door, he looked right at you, so I knew I wasn't seeing things." *What the fuck have I gotten myself into?*

"Let me guess: you must have thought that I was something foolish like a vampire or some other non-human supernatural creature. No, I'm real, and I do see my reflection in mirrors. You can feel the warmth of my hand on yours, can't you? Oh, before I forget: I want to thank you for bringing this to my attention. I was unaware I had this capability."

"But how did this happen to you?"

"Let's just say I had an operation that changed the course of my life for the better. I'm enhanced in ways you couldn't imagine. Now, my young stalker, what did you hope to gain by tracking me down and confronting me with this?"

"I was hoping maybe to learn how you could do this, maybe use you to enhance my career. Use what I learned about you to make you sleep with me. Fucking a woman as beautiful as you as young as I am would have been an awesome achievement for me." *What is making me tell her this. I didn't want to tell her that! Oh God, what have a I done!*

"I can see the worry in your eyes, and you have every reason to be terrified. The honesty with which you now speak is also my doing. Now, let me ask you a question. What made you think that you could possibly control someone who can do whatever it is you suspected about me?" Raven held up one of his photos.

"I don't know. I thought maybe however you did this would be something I could use. Anyone that can't be photographed wouldn't want the world to know, so I thought if I confronted you with it, I'd learn your secret."

"Ah, yes. I can see how you would jump to that conclusion. You made a comment earlier about not wanting my friends at the bar to become aware of your little discovery. Well, my young stalker, as far as that goes, I don't have any friends. Give me your phone and the video camera."

"Sure." He handed her his shoulder bag.

"This is what I can do to your head and all the bones in your body."

What the fuck! She crushed my phone with one hand, like it was made of paper. Shit. She's gonna fuckin' kill me.

"Please, Raven, you don't have to kill me. Why can't you just make me forget I ever saw you? Please make me forget about everything. No one will ever know."

She put his crushed phone in the bag.

Tears began to fall down his face.

"I'm afraid making you forget won't work," she said. "I can't take the chance that your memories may return. You see, when I push someone in this way, I usually kill them right away, so I don't know how long the effect will last. You may as well stop crying. It won't help you. Please wipe the water from your face. You're a grown little man, and it's embarrassing. So, among your many foolish motivations, you thought you'd somehow force me into having sex with you. That alone will increase the pleasure I will experience when I kill you. You see, among my other enhancements is a complete lack of empathy, and my favorite hobby now, my young stalker, is slaughtering people.

"Please. You don't have to do this to me. I'm really sorry. Please don't kill me," he begged. *Somebody, please help me. Please!*

"Oh, but I do and I am. Look into my eyes, Karson, and don't say a word. Place both hands on the table and interlace your fingers. That's a good boy. As your heart begins to beat faster, I want you to imagine what it would have been like to have sex with me. I want you to think about what other pleasures you might have enjoyed tonight, had you not tracked me down to extort favors from me. I want your heart to beat faster now. Maybe you'd be enjoying your girlfriend's company. Faster. Or that of a friend. Faster. Maybe watching a movie, or having a drink, or whatever it is you do for fun. Faster. I want your heart to beat even faster. Yes, I can see the veins and arteries in your face and neck start to bulge. Oh, poor baby. You're sweating profusely now. Faster. No, don't try to move your arms, and please try to control your trembling. I want your heart to beat faster. You're experiencing tachycardia. I can hear your heart pounding in your chest. I want you to know that your death is seconds away now. Faster. Beat faster. Do you feel the agony of death coming for you, Karson? Knowing that there is nothing you can do about it. Your young strong heart is about to give out on you. Can you feel it, Karson? Are you screaming in that warped little mind of yours? You are only seconds away from death."

Oh! . . . God! . . . Ahh! His head abruptly fell on top of his hands. Saliva poured from his mouth, and blood from his nose.

Raven stood and walked away. *That was most gratifying. Now I have much to consider.*

Epilogue 1

THE ELDERS ASSEMBLED in one of the vast science labs of Ogun's compound.

"My brothers," Ogun said. "Gather around and behold the thing for which we searched."

"So, this is the Homo we went through so much to capture. This one cost a trainload of Homos their lives. Looking at him now, in stasis, it hardly seems it was worth the effort."

"No, Shango," Ogun said, "it was indeed worth every effort. In the time he has been here, his genetic structure has been cataloged, and my scientists have completed a detailed analysis of every system in his body. I believe you all will find this most interesting. Doctor, report to the council your findings."

"The specimen, Jason Scot, was implanted with Leader Damon's kidneys. Before the organs were implanted, he suffered from a rare variety of the degenerative disease Parkinson's to such an extent he would have died far younger than would normally have been expected. His would have been a crippling, agonizing death. Approximately twenty weeks after his implantation, no signs of the chemical imbalances or the genetic markers for the disease remained in his body or brain.

"After we identified the specimen, we learned that the condition is inherent in his family, and his symptoms began to show far earlier than would be expected for a man his age. Our analysis revealed that the implanted kidneys, once separated from the rest of the body's Bio-Chemical Regenerative Glandular System, activated this Homos latent universal immune response. He would have undergone excruciating pain during that process. Together, these two once believed incompatible Bio/Chem systems, one primitive and one advanced, not only cured him of Parkinson's but also restructured his DNA.

"As he is now, in stasis, his heart and lung functions are twenty-seven percent more efficient than the average Homos of his age and sex. The interconnective tissues of his musculature are thirty-eight percent above Homo norms. Blood oxygenation, immune response, skeletal structure—all above current Homo norms. Physically, he is not on our level, but he is far above any Homo. The implanted Proto kidneys, however, have reverted to ordinary Homo norms. To survive in this Homo's body, without the rest of its natural systems, the advanced organs reverted to a form that would allow them to function in this Homo's body, while leaving his active immunity intact. However, the changes that were made in his body are permanent.

"Fascinating," Nuru said. "He is no longer purely Homo, nor is he Proto. He is now a hybrid. A living, functioning, hominid hybrid. Doctor, most hybrid species in nature cannot pass on their genetic traits. Could this Homo pass on these genetic anomalies?"

"If it is allowed to breed, all its newly acquired improvements would pass to its offspring," replied the doctor.

"Incredible," said Nuru.

"Then what we suspected was correct," Damon said. "The Homos Laden implanted with my organs did somehow mutate."

"Destroying the Homos on that train was the correct course of action," Shango insisted. "If this thing mutated in this way, it is possible that he could have developed other anomalies that could have affected other Homos simply by breathing the same air."

"You are both correct," the doctor agreed. "If you will observe the readouts of his blood analysis on the screen—" He pointed.

"Note that the L-9 factor in his system is off the charts," Ogun said. "If he were conscious, he'd be a raving lunatic. No Homo could control their impulses with levels that high. His urge to kill would be uncontrollable."

"That is correct," the doctor said. "The L-9 factor is present in a very select few Homos. Those that produce even the smallest amounts will become what their society dubs serial killers. Since our bodies don't produce L-9 factor, we haven't taken the time to study its effects in the quantities this specimen is producing, until now. Secreted from the primitive brain stem in Homos, the hormone causes catastrophic chemical imbalances in the brain that no Homo could control. This specimen's L-9 factor, while high even in stasis, is being neutralized to almost normal levels by his now active immunity. Nevertheless, he'd still morph into a mad killer if he were to rejoin his society."

"Doctor," Shango asked. "Do we know what this Homo looked like before his little transformation?"

"Yes, we do leader. If you will turn to the monitor."

All the elders present looked at the monitor and back to the man lying in front of them.

"This is an entirely different person," Nuru exclaimed. "This Homo is taller, younger, well built, and far heavier than his former self. He looks nothing like the Homo on the screen. Do we know what the other Homos looked like before their transformations?"

"Yes, leader," replied the doctor. "We have all the information on every patient Laden experimented on using Leader Damon's blood and organs. However, we don't know what they look like now. All but one of the transfused patients is dead."

"What do you mean all, but one is dead!" Damon pounded his fist on the table.

"Calm yourself, Damon," Ogun said. "We will get to that shortly." He turned to the doctor. "Doctor, take us to examination room two."

The elders followed the doctor in silence. Once in the exam room, they gathered around the body of what appeared to be a young woman.

"Leaders, this is Shelly Robinson," the doctor explained. "She was transfused with blood from Leader Damon. Of the transfused patients, only she survived. The others, Carl Petersen and Ricardo Williams, died after they murdered everyone around them. Our people were informed in the early stages of the investigation, when Carl Petersen's body was found. A policeman on the scene sent out over the air that he looked like a werewolf because his body was covered in what looked like fur. We had the bodies in our facilities shortly thereafter."

"Why is this one still alive?" asked Damon.

"Like the Homos that received your organs, leader," the doctor explained, "the three Homos that were given your blood were all suffering from genetic maladies of various types. Laden wanted to see if the immune factors in your blood would cure these Homos of their various conditions. It caused cataclysmic mutation. The foreign blood coursing through them triggered staggering levels of L-9 factors to be released into their bloodstreams, and ultimately that's what killed them. Without the Proto-Bio/chem organs to regulate the L-9 hormone, it triggered a metamorphosis in these Homos never seen before. In a matter of hours, they reverted to savage, primitive forms of non-Homo Sapien types. The changes made to this one's body should have killed her as well. Her skin pigmentation is permanently altered to the pale, chalky-white coloration you see before you. The same with the hair."

The doctor picked up a pair of forceps. "Leaders if you will note—"

"All its teeth are pointed," Shango said, "and the gums and tongue are black."

"This indicates that there is no blood circulating in its body," said Ogun. "There is also no respiration, yet the sensors show it is breathing."

"While it is in the stasis field, its body is immobile and almost dormant," the doctor said, "but note it's reaction to a change in condition. Computer, reduce lab lights by eighty percent." The lights dimmed to almost total darkness.

"Look, its eyes opened," said Damon. "Its bio readings are changing! It's regaining consciousness."

"Computer return lights to normal," the doctor ordered. "Note that the eyes are again closed, and its bio readings have returned to previous levels. This specimen is photosensitive to an unheard-of degree. If it were out of stasis and in low light, it would be a fully functioning sociopathic killer. This, leaders, is the result of L-9 factor unchecked in the Homo body, with the catalyst being the mutagenic effect of the Proto blood attempting to cure her genetic defects without the Protos Bio/Chem system. This Homo's current condition is also permanent. Before it was captured, it literally tore apart everyone in its household with its bare hands and teeth. When its body was scanned, its stomach was filled with human flesh and three distinct blood types. We surmise the specimen went into a dormant stage during daylight. When our people arrived on scene at its home, it was in a body bag. It began to move inside the bag, so our people placed it in stasis and transported it to a facility outside of Baltimore until it could be brought here."

"Has the analysis of the air sample taken from the scene of Senator Porter's murder been completed?" Shango asked.

"Yes, leader," the doctor replied, "and it's molecular structure revealed that the substance is a form of unknown pheromone with psychotropic properties. Such a substance has never been cataloged."

"Chief Scientist," Ogun asked, "have you learned all there is to know about these specimens?"

"Yes, leader. We have all the bio-samples we need, and extensive readings on both specimens."

"Excellent. I want them both destroyed immediately. We will return to my council chambers."

"It will be done, Leader Ogun," the chief scientist replied.

"THE COUNCIL IS NOW CONVENED," Ogun declared. "After hearing my chief scientist's report, what say you?"

The four seated figures were silent for several seconds.

"After hearing that report, brothers," said Shango, "and seeing the Homos that mutated as a result of Laden's experiments, coupled with Ogun's perceptions and the unknown pheromonal substance that's been discovered, I'm convinced that if those two Homos could mutate to such a degree, then it's possible for the remaining Homo female to have mutated into a Dark Mother or a variation of one. We must find and destroy the remaining two, and any Homos affected by them. We know these things are mad dog killers, so we investigate all such incidents, and they will lead us right to them."

"I agree, Destroyer," replied Nuru.

"I agree, Destroyer," replied Damon.

"Let it be done!" commanded Ogun.

Epilogue 2

*I*CHANGE AND GROW *stronger with each passing day, and so too does my hunger increase. I had no idea I could not be photographed or videotaped. I need to explore this newly manifested ability. As I sit in front of this monitor, I* see only the sofa I'm sitting on. Not even the clothes I'm wearing are visible. Therein lies a clue. I stand, and the indentation on the sofa is clearly visible. I move the sofa, and it is clearly seen moving. I throw a cushion at the monitor, and it is captured on the screen. I walk in front of the camera, and no image of me shows on the monitor. I stand in front of a mirror, and I see myself clearly. I must find out how I'm causing this effect. Let's see what happens when I turn out the lights and walk in front of the camera. I can cover great distances in seconds in the darkness. I can travel between cities in the blink of an eye, which will serve me well, although I'm still learning how to use this ability. Now that the room is totally dark, let's see what happens when I stand in front of the monitor. Interesting, very interesting indeed. Now, back to Kenji. He is more than he seems, so I must believe that there are more like him, though I have yet to encounter any more with his scent. That voice that invaded my mind did said there were others like me, but not like me. My prey has gotten more interesting. I will destroy every one of his kind I encounter. Whatever they are, they can't hide what they smell like, and they will never see me coming. It's time for Kenji and me to play a most deadly game.